Do Not Be a Gentleman When You Say Goodnight

Mitch Sisskind

Introduction by Amy Gerstler

The Song Cave

Published by The Song Cave
www.the-song-cave.com

Design and layout by Mary Austin Speaker

ISBN 978-0-9967786-4-0
Library of Congress Control Number: 2016955125

FIRST EDITION

Table of Contents

MITCH SISSKIND

If you consult the highest authorities on the matter and Google the term *Absurdist Fiction*, Wikipedia will fill you in on that noble genre's characteristics. You will learn, for example, that:

> common elements in absurdist fiction include satire, dark humor, incongruity, the abasement of reason, and controversy regarding the philosophical condition of being "nothing." Works of absurdist fiction often explore agnostic or nihilistic topics.

This is a right-on-the-money description of Mitch Sisskind's brilliant, brain-teasing fiction and his delightful poetry as well. But where, in the otherwise informative Wikipedia entry, is the requisite, slightly blurry photo of Mitch? Where's the crowd-sourced, compact bio of this great American satirist/absurdist? In other words, *Whither Mitch Sisskind, Wiki?* I am chagrined to report that Wikipedia divulges *nothing* on the subject of Mr. Sisskind or his hilarious, ultra-inventive, erudite, hyper-nimble fiction, under any heading *at all.* Nor does it utter a syllable, under many other available and eminently Sisskind-applicable headings, about his amazing, gymnastically imaginative poetry.

I'm sure you'll agree, dear reader, that *this is absurd,* right off the bat. Some of Mitch's colleagues in the black-humor biz, a selection of his comrades in bleak hilarity, do appear in the *absurdist fiction* article. This handful of Sisskind's fellow travelers across the parched sands of perfect deadpan, this cadre of brother reason-abasers, are acknowledged in the article, with bios, bibliographies and portraits. Interestingly, though, no Americans are mentioned, and no one who wrote absurd fiction *recently* shows up, either. All examples are from the distant past, way back before the internet was invented. Gogol, for example, is represented by a painting of his dashing Russian self clad in a white blouse with high, bandage-y collar, as though he's trying desperately to hide his neck. (There seem to be a *lot* of absurdist Russian writers. Perhaps Russians, like Americans, have an especially huge wealth of elements in their lives ripe to be satirized.) Eugene Ionesco, a pudgy, bald Frenchperson with sad, pouchy, basset hound eyes, is shown in an intentionally distorted headshot. It looks as though the photo was repeatedly sliced lengthwise and then pasted onto ill-aligned venetian blinds. Ionesco's face is thus fragmented to show us *just how absurd* a writer he is. Kafka also graces pages in Wikipedia's *absurdist fiction* entry, shy and stiff in his black bowler, wearing the quiet smile often seen on the lips of those who will die prematurely.

But as this complaint states, the Wikipedia article contains nary a peep about Sisskind, or *the Sisskindesque,* that literary term soon to dominate bookish conversations among serious readers in every city, village and town where vitally original satire and dark laughter are valued. Nor, for that matter, is there any mention in the Wikipedia piece of the man who was arguably Sisskind's closest American *absurdist fiction* kinsman, perhaps a cousin or uncle. That man was none other than Donald Barthelme.

Unlike the elusive Sisskind, Barthelme has his own Wikipedia page. Don B., as he was known to intimates, is depicted in his signature beard, sans moustache. Yet miraculously, he manages not to look Amish. He wears big, oddly shaped glasses which help identify him as an 80s-arty-intellectual rather than some humble Pennsylvania farmer who eschews buckles and zippers. The sly look on Barthelme's face hints that he's guarding heaps of amusing secrets.

When Barthelme died in 1989, at the age of 58, the *New Yorker,* where he had published frequently, wrote of his work:

> A typical Barthelme story was simultaneously . . . profound and hilarious, brief and long-term, trifling and heartbreaking. . . . [He] was variously summarized as an avant-gardist, a collagist, a minimalist, a Dadaist, an existentialist, and a postmodernist, but even a cursory re-reading of his work leaves one with the certainty that none of these narrowings are of much use.

Though, once again, this list of descriptions applies *so very, very aptly* to Mr. Sisskind's work, perhaps the anonymous scribe who wrote Barthelme's *New Yorker* obit was right. Perhaps amassing all these phrases and labels in an attempt to categorize Sisskind, to strap him into the straightjacket of historical context and terminology, and, indeed, perhaps even totting up the many Wikipedia articles *he needs to be featured in* based on the myriad genre terms that can and should be applied to his super smart, funny, one-of-a-kind writing may, in the end, be a fool's errand. Maybe trying to glue labels on this true American Literary Original, Mitch Sisskind, is like unto mixing up a crazy batch of alphabet soup, into which more and more terms are dumped willy-nilly, ad nauseum, till the bubbling cauldron is senselessly overflowing and making a soon-to-be-crusty mess on the stovetop, rather than shedding light on Sisskind's special genius for pastiche, his meditations on sexual sadness, the expert way he pitches clichés at the reader's head only to have them zoom 360 degrees around the readerly noggin and then come boomeranging back into his practiced hands, ready to be flung again. Maybe this labeling endeavor falls far short of properly honoring, for example, Sisskind's techniques for seamlessly interweaving the humdrum, the humiliating and the illuminatingly looney in ways that cause astonishment, giggles, a welling up of the tear glands, and quick versions of the adrenaline rush associated with roller coaster rides. Perhaps this pursuit of the perfect literary label for Sisskind is getting us nowhere. Yes, this seems to be the case. He is simply too unique. Like many of the best things in life, Sisskind's work is ultimately unclassifiable. Absurdist fiction-poet? Satirist-magic-realist? Dark fairy tale spinner? Old Testament stand-up comic? None of these terms seems to make even a small dent in pinning down the ineffable Sisskindesque.

Before throwing up our hands and abandoning the topic of labels entirely, it may be important to say a quick word about Sisskind's own deployment of names. He is interested in names as life-complication, burden, fate-determiner, millstone around the neck, or plain zany moniker. Dogs named Matzoh, Vegetable, Grandpa Munster and Monster Man appear in the volume you now have in your hands. Ditto a massage parlor cat named Gross Out, who rudely refuses to collude with a sad, damaged man, a regular at said massage parlor, when said man attempts to show off to his favorite masseuse by proving he has the power to communicate with animals, which in fact, he has. But the maddening cat won't play ball, won't speak to him, until the woman leaves the room. Recognizing Sisskind's ability to integrate verisimilitude and the implausible world of the absurd in pursuit of higher truths, we may exclaim, when we read this story, *Yes! Cats are exactly like that!*

Sisskind's names for humans are often a bit more awkward, ridiculous and borderline unpronounceable than his names for animals. This seems accurate, and indicative of the ways these two types of creatures navigate the world. Humans bumble. Animals know better. When you read Mr. Sisskind, men with names like Steve Tomato, Moe Kelp, Manny Organic, Rabbi Michael Mushnik, Peklar Jenknavorian, and Hub Snell may be found chowing down at Belden Corned Beef Center. In Sisskind's stories and poems, you will also make the acquaintance of dames named Tuba, Tokyo Lipscomb, Fawn Nisner, Birdie Uberflussig, and more. One Sisskind fable about the vagaries of naming begins, "His family name was Goomniak but at fifty he changed it to Freed. Why Freed? Because he was *freed* of the name Goomniak." At the close of a poem about the power of names to shape fate in the sports and business worlds (spoiler alert!) the speaker re-christens himself *Duke Rhino* as a way of trying to rise beyond his lowly station in life.

Sisskind has a special love for the pathetic, the downtrodden, the regular Jane and Joe, for the redemptions and debasements in lives of deafening ordinariness. And he is always able to reveal the bright or plodding oddnesses in these lives. Human dignity and its glaring absence are also big Sisskind themes, in keeping with his rep as a card-carrying absurdist who traffics in the particularly American conundrums of wanting to be a *somebody* while being made to feel like you're *nothing.* Sometimes the messed up and the meek are exalted in Sisskind's work. Perhaps just as often in the Sisskind universe, both the puffed up *and* the deflated among us are squashed under the grinding heel of circumstance, and usually that circumstance is of a surreal, divine and/or crazily imaginative order. Sisskind's brand of "gentle anti-realism" (a term used by Sarah Manguso to describe the fabulist prose poems of Russell Edson, another writer Sisskind's work has big affinities with) is not always so gentle. Sure, humor tempers the darkness in his work, but often enough in Sisskind stories, everyone's buzz gets majorly harshed. That's nihilism for you—an equal opportunity oppressor. Often in the Sisskindesque world, despite fantastical twists and turns, everyone is a loser. None of us remains unscathed, talking animals notwithstanding.

When you read some Sisskind stories, you may think of James M. Cain, despite the fact that Sisskind is a million times more playful than Cain.

The Sisskind story "The Death of Molesworth" in particular lifts and twists plot and character elements from *Double Indemnity* and *The Postman Always Rings Twice.* For example, the story mixes Cain's atmosphere of gritty desperation with Sisskind's fascination with dog fighting. Sisskind's send-up/homage to Cain borrows Cain's tropes of the murderous, greedy, oversexed young wife saddled with a rich, decrepit husband she'd just as soon be rid of. As in Cain's novels, a younger, laconic handyman lover is caught in the middle. Sisskind even calls the handyman guy in his story "Neff," a neat tip of the hat to "Walter Neff," portrayed in the film of *Double Indemnity* by Fred MacMurray. Mitch's story rethinks Cain's hardboiled, noirish ravenousness in strange and startling ways Cain never dreamed of.

Sisskind's frequent and actually learned use of Judaica is also notable. In his poem "Resolution and Independence," a dark comic elegy to a homeless man whose "companion was a chicken," Sisskind mixes formal and informal poetic diction to wonderful effect. When the police arrest the harmless, homeless gent, he merely laughs and says, "Mene mene tekel upharsin." This is not an example of the so-called word salad one sometimes hears dribble from the mouths of untreated, vagrant schizophrenics but is in fact a quote from the Book of Daniel, and a moving and appropriate quip in context. Sisskind has the homeless man hassled by cops quote the divine handwriting that appears on a wall at King Belshazzar's feast, containing an ominous prophesy: "God has numbered the days of your reign and brought it to an end. You have been weighed on the scales and found wanting. Your kingdom is divided and given to your rivals." This is roughly the way Daniel translates it in the Old Testament. What better way to speak truth to cruel, misused power? Sisskind is able to wield Yiddish in penetrating and comic ways. I can always make myself laugh by re-reading the first line of Sisskind's novella of a poem "Leo Manasin," which introduces his protagonist thusly: "Drilled through the *kishkes* in '44. . . ."

Sex and God are important in Sisskind land, powerful, yet also fallible and consistently delivering mixed messages. Sex and the divine are sometimes intertwined, seeming to be manifestations of the same irresistible force. Yet God and sex, for Sisskind, are at best fickle masters. Here is the opening of "Proposal and Disposal," in which God reveals himself to be an uptight, clumsy matchmaker:

> God saw that Lauren had been living with Frank for almost two years. He wanted them to get married, but when Frank proposed, Lauren hesitated. God decided to give her some encouragement using the telephone and telephone answering machine. . . .

"The Devotions of Jean Blysema" focusses on a guilt-ridden yet truly innocent woman who feels she has indulged in sexual immorality. She struggles to come to terms with her actions via a one-sided epistolary relationship with God. The story "I'm Stupid and My Wife Is Stupid," which originally appeared in *Playboy* magazine, can be read as an inventive reimagining of the annunciation.

In conclusion, a word about Sisskind's endings. Blessedly, Mitch is not going to teach you a lesson or present you with a canned moral, though his poems and stories deal with mores and wrestle with consequences, both real and utterly fantastical, and his writing has fable-like aspects. Rather than any neat solution or summing up, his stories and poems conclude on notes of confusion, equivocation, surprise, retraction, abruptness, or silence. Sisskind is a postmodern master of the anti-epiphany.

And finally, in the last sentences of this introduction, let me plead: *Wikipedia, do the right thing! Get with it! Post some Mitch Sisskind pages before this book hits its second printing!*

AMY GERSTLER

2016

Proposal and Disposal

God saw that Lauren had been living with Frank for almost two years. He wanted them to get married, but when Frank proposed, Lauren hesitated. God decided to give her some encouragement using the telephone and the telephone answering machine; the power of the written word; Fawn Nisner, who had once been Lauren's roommate; and Harry duCrowe, who had preceded Frank as Lauren's boyfriend. God hoped that this would solve the problem. He also knew that, if it didn't, He certainly had other means at His disposal.

When the telephone rang, Lauren, who was working, decided to let the machine take it. With the volume turned all the way up on the machine in the bedroom, she could hear who was calling even in the little room that served as her studio. In a moment Harry's amplified voice sounded through the apartment. Lauren stopped putting finishing touches on her cat painting and stared gloomily out the window, where a fog covered the suburban landscape.

"Hi, Laur, it's Harry. I'm in town for a day or so and I'd really like to see you, but the problem is that I don't have a car, so I'm completely dependent on Ralph. But I'm actually going to be near you in an hour or so, so if you're going to be there maybe I could just drop by, providing it wouldn't cause any *sturm und drang*. I'll give you a call in about an hour. Hope you're around. 'Bye."

Lauren chewed on a strand of her hair and felt her palms begin to sweat. Suddenly she felt trapped in this town, in this country, even in this world, knowing that Harry was back. On the other hand, it was kind of good to hear his voice after so long. Sometimes when Lauren was nervous she threw up. She walked to the bathroom, but nothing happened. Then the doorbell rang.

As Vegetable, Frank's dog, barked furiously, Lauren reasoned that it couldn't be Harry at the door, based on what he'd said to the answering machine. But she also knew that years of studying such insects as the ant lion had taught Harry something about deviousness. Finally she walked quietly to the door and looked through the peephole. It was not Harry, it was Fawn. Lauren opened the door.

Vegetable jumped happily at Fawn, but the young woman brushed him aside. Fawn, who often seemed miserable, now appeared even more depressed than usual. Her head was cocked sideways above a mouse-colored dress as she pleaded, "Mind if I come in?" She and Lauren kissed and hugged.

Though concerned about the Harry situation, Lauren said, "Believe it or not, I've just been trying to get some work done. But I'd love your company." She led Fawn through the apartment to the studio.

There the visitor smiled in admiration of the painting and declared, "I love what you're doing with that feline shape." She traced the outline of a cat in the air.

Lauren sighed, "Maybe in another life I can be a really talented person."

"You are a really talented person, and you know it," Fawn said.

"I'm not."

"Well, isn't being beautiful enough?"

Lauren was silent. She dropped a paintbrush in a jar of turpentine and said, "I'm going to make some tea. We can sit and talk."

"I didn't mean to interrupt your painting. It's just that. . ."

"You didn't interrupt it. I'm finished for today. Let's have some tea."

"I didn't mean anything by . . . it's just that . . ."

"Let's have some tea."

"Okay."

Then, as Lauren put things away, Fawn, who worked as a grade-school art teacher, bent close to the painting, pointed to a tiny figure in the corner, and asked, "What's that?"

"It's supposed to be Vegetable. I'm doing this picture for Janice and Jim because he chased their cat up a tree. The cat is big and the dog is small. It's a cat's idea of a better world."

"But you can hardly make out that it's a dog," Fawn half-giggled, half-whined. Turning, she remarked, "I understand Harry is in Cambridge," but Lauren had already gone out of the studio.

Sitting at the dining room table, Fawn looked hard at her friend and declared, "You're wondering why I'm not in school."

"I thought it must be a holiday."

"It's no holiday, babe. I did something Tuesday that I guess I'm not proud of, but it was to survive in that jungle they call an art room. I scotch-taped a couple of kids' mouths shut and one of them blabbed to mommy. Some sort of administrative procedure has been started against me and meanwhile I've been banished from the classroom."

"How awful!" Lauren said, but Fawn raised a hand for silence.

"Some good may come of it," she intoned. "I've made a decision that I want to tell you about. I want to preface it, though, with a few admissions that may come as a surprise to you."

At that moment the telephone rang. Fawn's face showed annoyance as Lauren stood up from the table and said, "Maybe I'd better get that."

"Can't the machine do it?" In fact, Lauren's recorded voice could already be heard from the bedroom, apologizing, hoping for a message, and so on and so forth.

But the live Lauren only assured Fawn, "Believe me, I really want to hear about this. I really do. It's just that I'm expecting a call." Then she disappeared into the bedroom and closed the door behind her.

"Laur? Laur? Oh, hi again," said Harry, as she picked up the receiver just after the beep. His cheerful tone surprised Lauren, even disappointed her. From their last conversation, now almost three years ago, she recalled the desperate strength of his pleas, accusations, promises, and excuses, like a drowning man's. But Lauren's own voice surprised her as well.

"Hi, stranger. Where are you?"

"Well, I've got some tough news. Ralph's car broke down so we're stuck here, and I'm seeing Wilson at one. I really wanted to talk to you, though, if only telephonically," Harry laughed. "I'm at a pay phone so we've only got three minutes."

Lauren looked at the clock beside the bed. "Let me call you back, then."

"It's no good, Laur. Time is short."

As Harry took a deep breath, and exhaled into the receiver, Lauren tried to imagine him standing at the payphone. Even that seemed almost adulterous here in the room she shared with Frank, where a kind of whimsical domesticity had been cultivated. A plush rhinoceros, three feet long, lay upside down on the foot of the bed.

"Well, it's been a long time," Lauren said. "How have things been going?"

"You mean what have I been working on? I feel really funny about it, but I'm obsessed with the sphex."

"The sphex?"

"Yeah. And I know what you're thinking. I like to say that the sphex flies in the face of all my principles. Ho, ho, ho, right? I mean, I guess I've gotten away from the whole political thing that attracted me to entomology in the first place, the notion of materialist struggle taking place in the insect world with an analysis to be drawn from it. Remember when roaches used to be my thing?"

"I suppose we've all changed," Lauren said, feeling funny.

"Remember when you used to love me for it?"

"Well, not really for that."

"For what, then?"

Lauren hesitated. What was a sphex? And what had she loved about Harry? It seemed impossible to remember now in the middle of this conversation, which seemed close to taking an unpleasant turn. Perhaps it had been the way he threw perfect spirals with the Nerf football, when they used to play catch in the park. Once, Lauren remembered, she had praised him for that, and he'd looked so pleased.

"*For what, then?*"

"Harry . . ."

"Okay, sorry. Didn't mean to put you on the witness stand." But, suddenly, his cheerfulness was gone. In an urgent voice Harry said, "Listen, and there's something I want to say. A man and a woman living together out of wedlock is wrong. I don't know much about Frank, but I believe you should get married to him, that you should bear his children, and that you should raise them up straight and tall. Anything else is a cop-out, Lauren. Let me put it this way: you can't keep a promise you never made."

Even if she'd had something to say, Lauren could not have replied to this. The connection was suddenly broken. The time was up. Frowning, puzzled, she took a moment to compose herself before facing Fawn again.

But Fawn was not there. Where she had been sitting, a note lay on the table:

Lauren—

Obviously you had something very important to talk about with someone, but since I had something very important to talk about with you my feelings were hurt and I just decided to leave. You see, I'm tired of being the jolly slob that everybody likes (except herself) and my leaving will show you that I'm going to change. Oh yes, you're probably wondering what I was going to tell you, which happens to be that I am going to have my jaws wired shut for as long—although I'm not overweight—for as it takes to acquire an absolutely beautiful body. Yes, one that may be even more beautiful than yours, Lauren, because I too want to have long nights of sex such as I'm sure you've had many of in your life, but such as I've had none of because I've always been me. One other thing. I think you should get married to Frank if he has asked you, which would not surprise me, and that you are asking for trouble if you don't. Just living together seems oh so easy, and marriage is difficult, I'm sure, but isn't there an old saying that she who bears the greatest burden shall know the greatest truth? I still consider you my friend.

Fawn

Lauren dropped the note. She felt hurt, as if she wanted to cry, but angry, too. She felt angry with the collection of misfits from her past. She touched the teapot, found that it was still warm, and started to fill her cup. But then she turned and walked back into the bedroom.

Lying on the bed, Lauren rested her feet on the rhinoceros. She stared at the ceiling with its thousands of little stucco points, which now disgusted her. Closing her eyes, she tried to think of Colorado, where she and Frank had walked along a beautiful trail holding hands, and how they had seen a coyote. Lauren had been wearing her new red t-shirt, and Frank had a beard then. He only had it for a couple of weeks. Frank, Colorado, the t-shirt, the coyote, these are on one side, Lauren thought. Harry and Fawn, they're on the other side—but perhaps they were right about just one thing. Lauren knew that if Frank walked into the apartment at that very moment she would agree to marry him. It was what God had been waiting for. He rearranged things so that Frank had actually left work forty-five minutes earlier. Just then Vegetable barked excitedly as Frank's key unlocked the door.

Yet sometimes God feels worse than ever after He's gotten His way. Now He said, "I've been unbelievably slack about things for a long time. But it all seems like such a vicious circle, such a never-ending cycle."

1981

Iliad

Old age, Tolstoy wrote, is the biggest surprise
In a man's life. So true! Childhood hours
In the ancient car I now recall, the hot months,
Sox game on the radio, soporific Bob Elson
Mumbling in the microphone, "Um, strike one,"
And at bat Sherman Lollar, sloth-like catcher,
Elson droning, "Ball four. It's a base on balls,"
Henri Bergson called this perceived duration,
The sense of time as elastic phenomenon
Stretched or compressed by stoic's fortitude
Or child's impatience: "Are we there yet?"
And this is where the surprise comes in.
Yes, my good man, you have arrived *there.*
Yes, you are *there* all right, ya big dummy.

In fact, you've already been *there* for a while
Except "there" is not "where" or even "what"
You would have imagined. "There" is "here,"
Wherever you happen to be at the time.
As the snail everywhere bears its shell,
You and the destination are one now, not
Where you're going but what you are.

But we will grieve not, as Wordsworth wrote.
Or perhaps we will grieve. Shall we? No matter,

It doesn't really amount to a hill of beans.
That's just how the cookie crumbles,
That was the funeral of Hector.

2014

A Mean Teacher

There was no chalk in Miss Carter's room. It was gone. She wanted to write on the blackboard. I'll send a child to Miss Baylie's room, thought Miss Carter, to get some chalk.

Still, she remembered: Miss Baylie is like an elephant. Who shall I send there, she wondered.

There were no troublemakers.

The children sat in blue desks, thinking: There is such a thing as ghosts. They read of other lands.

"All right, Paula," said Miss Carter. "Four times eight." "Four times eight," Paula said. "Thirty-two. You scared me." There was a general flying laugh. At that Miss Carter changed colors.

"Less noise, if I were you," she said. "Maurice, give me five times eight plus three times eight, in your head. You had better know the eights, my friend."

"Three times eight," said the boy. "Twenty-four. Sixty-four, I guess it is," he said, thinking: I have nothing to be ashamed of.

Outside mothers pushed their babies past the school. The pupils heard them crying in their carriages. And safes fell on those carriages in Miss Carter's mind.

"Maurice," she said. "Can a man on foot escape an elephant?"

They look slow, thought Maurice, but they are not.

"No," he said. "They look slow, but they're too big. Why, with one step of their giant legs—"

He was humiliated quickly.

“The answer is sometimes!” shouted the children. “It says in the book sometimes you can: Bumba was chased by one!” In their minds men were escaping.

Miss Carter roamed the front of the room. There was her hair, the color of a radiator. Then there were her metal lips.

“Maurice,” she said, “go down to Miss Baylie’s room and ask nicely if you may borrow some chalk.”

Maurice was fat yet loved to hum when he ran. This makes it like a movie, he would think. But he walked quietly down the hall to Miss Baylie’s room and knocked on the door.

“Come in,” said Miss Baylie. Maurice opened the door, thinking: She is more like the dinosaurs. There were the big kids, so awful.

“I’m sorry to bother you, Miss Baylie,” Maurice said. “But Miss Carter would like to borrow some chalk.”

A mean teacher, Miss Baylie took the boy into her cloakroom, a belly. She beat him up there, asking: “How would you like to go down to the office, and see Mr. Wadsworth?” Outside some laughed to hear the thuds. “My glasses, my glasses!” shouted Maurice, in her clutches. “Really, it’s hilarious, Charlie,” said a big kid girl, and whispered: “From inside there she can’t see us, darling.” “Let me take you to the land of dreams,” responded a young man. That night Maurice told his mother what had happened.

What kind of woman is Miss Baylie, anyway, she wondered. Where does she come from?

Miss Baylie lived with her father Jake. She had become a big fat one through the years.

When Miss Baylie was small her parents would walk with her around the block. In those days her mother would hold the right hand, and her father would hold the left hand. Those were the days, too, of her mother's strange infection. Those were the days that Jake was out of a job. Once an old man approached him.

"I'm not going to tell you a long story," said the old man. "I want a quarter for a drink of whiskey."

"I just don't have a quarter to give you," Miss Baylie's father told him. He put one hand on the old man's shoulder. "I just haven't got it. I'm out of a job."

"Then we part friends," said the bum, moving along. They heard his spitting. Just then Miss Baylie's mother made some noise: she claimed her whole body itched. One day her life collapsed like a chair.

"We have to be brave," said Jake, thinking: I've got to find a job. Then he found one.

With time things became easier for Miss Baylie and her father. They moved to a neighborhood where the dogs were not quite lovely collies, but neither were they chows. And on Sundays when Miss Baylie and Jake walked around the block he no longer held her hand, but it was displayed for all the passersby. And they thought: So light brown! One day an old man approached Miss Baylie's father.

"Give me this moist daughter of yours," he shouted, his arms on her shoulders, her face in his mouth. Miss Baylie covered the man with punches.

"All right, mister," said Jake. "Okay for you." This is no fun, the bum thought. He forgot about the whole idea.

It was a hot day for April. The trees made short shadows on the sidewalk. Because it is almost noon, thought Miss Baylie. But then: I hate that old man, whose lips dripped. They went ahead.

"Well, what do you want to do with your life," Jake asked. "Say, I hope you're not hurt."

"Be a teacher," said Miss Baylie.

"That's a good idea," her father said. Yet one day he would rip her heart out and eat it. One day Miss Baylie would turn around and she would be shaped differently. Then Jake would ask: "How was work today? Well, I know there's nothing wrong with working for a while when you're eighteen or nineteen years old. All the girls get jobs in banks, or they become secretaries, or they become teachers. But they don't just let themselves go! You just let yourself go! By the time a girl is twenty-five she's married, and has a girl of her own. And believe me by the time she's thirty-five she's mighty glad to have the children around; they bring some cheerfulness into her life. Do you think movie actresses don't have kids? Well, sometimes the studio doesn't want the public to know how many kids an actress has because it might make her look like an old woman to some people. Listen, every one of those actresses has plenty of kids! Do they know how long their careers are going to last? How do they know when some young actress is going to come along and steal the audience? And a lot of them get killed in accidents. But one thing is for sure: no matter what happens, they've left some kids to carry on, and provide them with grandchildren if they're still here. And most of the time, if the mother was a beautiful actress, the daughter will turn out to be beautiful and probably will go into acting herself, or if it's a son he'll be a handsome actor. And neither of them will have very much trouble getting married and providing a few kids, that's all I know. Well, I could stand to hear the laughter of children again. Is it too late? What's your plan?" "I don't feel well," Miss Baylie would say. "Shut up."

Maurice's mother grabbed her son and went to see Mr. Wadsworth, saying, "You're the principal, aren't you?"

"Why yes," said Mr. Wadsworth. He listened to her organ recital. Then he sent for Miss Baylie; she appeared at his door.

"Come in, Miss Baylie," said Mr. Wadsworth. "This is Mrs. Minor. I gather you know Maurice."

"Yes," said Miss Baylie.

"And in fact Maurice has a lot to do with my asking you to come down here this morning," Mr. Wadsworth said. "That is, it concerns your relationship with Maurice. Now correct me if I'm wrong, but this seems to be the situation: last night the boy here told his mother that he'd come into your room on an errand from Miss Carter and that you took him into the cloak room and punched him. Is that right, Maurice?"

"Yes, Mr. Wadsworth," he said.

"Now then. Miss Baylie, what's your side of the story?"

"Sir," Miss Baylie said, "I was trying to conduct a class, and I was interrupted. I don't mind, of course, as long as the child is a gentleman. But I'm afraid . . ."

"Is that the kind of school I'm sending my son to?" asked

Mrs. Minor. "Is that the kind of thing that goes on?" Once she had witnessed the beating of a horse.

"Now Maurice, did you provoke Miss Baylie in any way?" Mr. Wadsworth asked. "Did you knock on the door?"

"No . . . yes," said Maurice. Suddenly he burst into tears. "Yes, I did. She knows I knocked, too. She might not say so." His mother flew to him.

"You see, Miss Baylie," Mr. Wadsworth said, "this kind of thing creates a lot of problems. And really, is there any excuse for it?" He studied his folded hands. "Now I want to make myself crystal clear. We cannot—"

"Excuse me, Mr. Wadsworth! Excuse me!" said Miss Baylie, standing up.

"Now don't get upset," Mr. Wadsworth said. "I'd imagine there are enough people upset already, wouldn't you say? Well then."

"It's not that," said Miss Baylie. "It's just that my body has begun to itch. It's happened before. But . . ."

"Itch?" sobbed Maurice.

"Now, Miss Baylie . . ." said Mr. Wadsworth.

"It's all right," Miss Baylie said, sitting down. "Pardon me."

"Well, as I was about to say . . ." Mr. Wadsworth continued.

"Just one thing!" Miss Baylie burst out. "I know the children dislike me. I know they tell their parents about me, and make jokes about me. I don't need to be told that. But I want one thing to be clear: whatever I did, it was to help them. I knew they would often misunderstand, and be hurt, but I hoped that someday in the future it would become clear to them, that someday they would think kindly of me, or—if not that—at least remember me. I felt I owed them something which no one else seems prepared to give—the feeling that what they do is important, that it makes a difference whether even a child acts rightly or wrongly, that there is such a thing as right and wrong. What does a child see when he looks about him in today's world? He sees adults abdicating their responsibilities to him, perhaps with the best of intentions but often with the worst possible results. He sees parents who so misunderstand love as to think it can only find expression in the gift of a new whistle of some sort, or in the decision *not* to administer a well-deserved beating. Today's are parents who fail to realize that the sowing in a child of integrity and self-denial will reap rich harvest long after the sting of a good crack in the mouth has been forgotten. But we have denied our children the pleasures—for they are pleasures, finally—of receiving these gifts, and hence we have denied ourselves the perhaps equally great pleasures of bestowing them. For the parents of today, seeking to retain for themselves the careless freedoms of childhood have thereby forfeited the satisfactions of seeing their sons and daughters grow into real men and women, real mothers and fathers of whom they can be proud. It is the irony of today's parent, who believes that to make one's child happy one need only remain ever a child oneself, to have brought down upon the young people exactly that uncertainty, even panic perhaps, which was presumably to be avoided. Can we imagine a generation more filled with doubt than that growing up today? It looks to its elders for guidance and finds only a few more 'pals.' And if the parents don't care, or care only in the wrong way, where can the children turn? The church, all the churches—with variations according to the degree that fashion has replaced principle in one or another of them—have simply followed the prevailing winds. So from the pulpits come only talk and more talk about the latest miracles—of the cinema, that is—or of the trash which has most recently fought its way to the top of the best-seller lists. And *what of* the writers? *What of* the artists? Have they moved to fill the blank sheet of paper, the empty canvas which is conscience in our time? The answer is no. No, they have decided to go on painting and writing and filming only whatever is least worthwhile and filthiest. But what a moment for poets and painters, and especially for the motion picture colony, to disdain even one more tasteless fling in the hay in favor of reminding us of those values which we have so utterly forgotten, yet seem ever the more trying to forget: the sunset over Hawaii, a bear trapping salmon in our Pacific Northwest. Indeed, things are at such a pass that the moment has traveled through ripeness into urgency, the opportunity having grown into a responsibility. It is this kind of responsibility that I have felt as a teacher, and it is this sense of urgency that has compelled me to act as I have. I can only wish it felt by every child's hero who is tempted to throw the big ball game, by every hunter who decides on just one pheasant over the limit, by every bride and groom who might then feel each other's kisses not simply in a spirit of whoop-jamboreehoo, but thinking: 'Will tonight bring a child into the world?'"

And the next moment she knelt before God's throne.

Mr. Wadsworth hurried to her side, and knelt to take her pulse. "Miss Baylie!" he shouted.

"Will she be all right?" asked Mrs. Minor, thinking: She grew too fat.

"It's no use," Mr. Wadsworth said. When the ambulance arrived he told them, "There is nothing more to be done."

"Of course not," said a young doctor. "Not as far as the woman herself is concerned. But a good autopsy may teach us things that will help in the future, and not just in cases like hers. We learn a lot."

"I don't understand it," Mr. Wadsworth said. "She'd never missed even a day of work, and then this. And then this."

"Well, from what you've told me," said the doctor, "it certainly sounds like the big itch. And if, as I suspect it will, a talk with the family shows there to be a history, well . . ."

"I'm closing the school," said Mr. Wadsworth. "I have no stomach for any more school today."

The children filed into the assembly hall. They knew something was up.

They thought: This is a special assembly.

"No talking," said Miss Carter. "For the first one who talks there is the furnace. Who will that be?"

Mr. Wadsworth rose slowly, carrying his body like a piano. "There will be no more school today," he said. "You see, Miss Baylie has suddenly passed away. Now, I don't know if you can understand . . . but I want you to understand. Oh, she's dead, she's fallen down that elevator shaft! And the cables gave way one after the other, and we may wonder, many of us, 'Mightn't she have grabbed something on the way down? Aren't the springs down there?' But it only remains for us to stare down the hole." There was some noise. "Listen, she gave something to you. In ten years you'll know what it was. As for now . . . well, what does a fish know about the water?" He unbuttoned his coat. "You'll know what she gave you when you move into high school, and go on to college. She always gave one-hundred-and-ten percent." Mr. Wadsworth rebuttoned his coat. That felt good. "She was always ready to lend a hand—be it in the lunch room, or on Work Day, or on Stupid Day, or for graduation: Miss Baylie." There was a quiet moment. "And now you may silently go. I expect the older ones to keep an eye on the younger ones."

The school opened like a can. It was near the end of May. Outside the children went to the park, hid in dark alleys, carried one another's books in kindness. Soon each would be in a different grade. One thought: Hooray. Boo-hoo, thought another. In the park many were attracted to the interesting flies eating a doodie. "That's human," they said. "There's no dog big enough to make that." "Of course there is," one said. Blocks away a big kid decided: I'll throw Kathleen's homework high in the air. "Awk!" said the girl. "Now I'm going to start kissing you," he said, thinking: This is Sergeant Rock, and we're moving into enemy territory. She thought, dreamland.

1968

Possum

At night occasionally a possum
Passes by peering in the window.
It represents my sexuality. Prehistoric,
Very slow moving, and the children
Would be repulsed by it were
They awake, which they are not.

Over time I begin to wait for it.
Was it attracted by the room's light
Or the murmuring television—
Who knows? No way to tell
What a possum is thinking or
At least that gift is not given to me.

I watch "Survivor." But the skittish
Marsupial now owns my waking thoughts
And later, brazenly, my dreams:
I climb a tall tree with it, we read
Comic books together: Donald Duck,
Scrooge McDuck, Daffy Duck, all the rest.

2009

It So Happens

I'm not bad looking, I'm not good looking. I'm average. I've got a regular body and a regular face, but I shall soon blossom. When I blossom I want to look like Jacqueline Bisset, who happens to be a woman with many supernatural powers and who is sort-of my fairy godmother.

When Jacqueline Bisset becomes extremely interested in a person she starts appearing to that person in the middle of the night. It's like a dream but it isn't, because when she sits on the edge of the bed you can see all the hairs and freckles on her arms and you can even feel the warmth of her skin, which doesn't happen in dreams. Usually she wears casual but chic sport clothes in blues, browns, or beiges and very little jewelry or makeup, because who needs it, anyway? On the first night she told how she had been watching me and how she cared about me a lot, which was really great except that I wanted to talk about her. At last the cat no longer had my tongue and I asked, "What's it like being beautiful and famous?"

Jacqueline Bisset sighed deeply and said, "First of all, there are beautiful women working at supermarket checkout counters, and then there are famous women who are not beautiful. But to be both at the same time makes you want to choose your projects very carefully, teaches you to look closely at the track records of the people you get involved with, and forces you to be awfully selective about your endorsements. Ah, me! If I had paid closer attention in some of these areas, my career might have turned out even bigger than it is. From now on I'm going to be making more of my own decisions instead of leaving everything up to the people who are handling me."

I realized that Jacqueline Bisset is just a normal person who can have the giggles or be depressed, who can talk stupid or talk serious. She will not talk dirty, however. Well, so much for the first visit of this celebrity. About a week later she arrived again.

I was sound asleep, but she shook me and said, "Allison, Allison." Finally I turned over and I really was not at all surprised to see her. We discussed Hollywood for a while until she announced, "Honey, there is a movie star that's crazy about you."

"Who is this movie star?"

"I promised him not to tell. You've got to be patient for the time being. The poor man wants to make love with you very much just for your personality, but he is also waiting and hoping for your beautiful, not overly large breasts, your legs that will be long and athletic, and your sexy ass. He has a girlfriend now, of course, but you'll easily take him away with these wonderful five things."

"Well, I have a boyfriend, too," I informed Ms. Bisset.

She said, "I know it. His name is Michael Minkus. Here is my advice. You should practice on Michael Minkus but do not become extremely involved with him, and meanwhile divide everything up into your schoolwork or your social life. Until you blossom, concentrate very hard on your schoolwork. Then, as soon as this process is finally completed, compare yourself with the other girls. If you think you've got them beat, become a sex maniac with anyone your heart desires. But if you really and honestly think you have got them beat *by a mile*, then you are going to be a world-famous actress. You should stop paying attention to your schoolwork, you should join the drama club. However, Allison, if you turn sixteen years old and you still think you haven't blossomed, forget about it because you actually have as much as you're ever going to. Simply admit this to yourself. Then decide if you might be someone who is skinny but with a lot of pizzazz to make up for it. If the answer is yes, join the drama club. But even if the answer is no, you can still be the brain of the class if you've been studying hard like I told you to."

That was Jacqueline Bisset's second visit. We then began getting together several times a week. Of course, there are probably a number of people who won't believe what I have said, or what I am going to say. Well, tough! Tough! Or, rather, that is alright. I will calmly prove it to you.

Last night I said to Jacqueline Bisset, "I love talking to you and you're my best friend, but when I'm in school or on the nights you're not here I feel worried sometimes. I know you're not a dream, but I'm afraid you might be just my imagination. I mean, how do you get back and forth between here and California, how do you sneak into my room without anyone seeing you, and other things, also?"

She smiled, squeezed both my hands, and whispered, "I know how alone you feel when I'm not with you, but try to remember that I never stop thinking about you. Anyway, I'm not always in Hollywood because my career takes me all over the world. When a woman becomes beautiful beyond a certain point, Allison, she is able to fly. She can walk through walls, speak the language of whatever country she is in, have X-ray vision, and communicate with animals. It's a really wild, really fantastic life. But you must rest now, my darling, because you're at a stage when rest is extremely important, and I'll be with you again soon."

She gave me a kiss and I closed my eyes. But I had this feeling that something was going to happen. Like, maybe, a bright light would fill the room, rock-and-roll music would start to play, and a magical cloud would change Jacqueline Bisset into a man and this man would be the mystery movie star who's in love with me. Too bad, but this did not take place.

Then when I woke up this morning I had this feeling that at last I might have blossomed. However, I found my same old self.

I got depressed. I thought, "Maybe after all it was a figment of your imagination."

But just then, under my pillow, I discovered a black matchbox. It is from The Bistro, 246 Canon Drive, Beverly Hills, CA. And it so happens that I have never been to California in my life.

1983

Then All Hell Breaks Loose: Thirteen Films of Tokyo Lipscomb

DEAD AS A DORMOUSE

Tokyo Lipscomb, a third-year student at Penn, and a few other girls move into a new apartment and find themselves next door to a burned-out ex-ballplayer named George Henry. Neighbors insist that George Henry vanished ten years earlier—but remember, Tokyo Lipscomb and the other girls are living next door to him. At the end we find out that Tokyo Lipscomb and the other girls are actually dead. They died in a car accident. But they come back to life with the help of George Henry. But he was also dead and stays dead. Then all hell breaks loose.

THE KEY

George Henry is a burned-out ex-ballplayer whose own face gets stuck after warning his daughters that their faces might get stuck if they make chipmunk faces. Tokyo Lipscomb, a third-year student at Penn, is assigned to write a paper about George Henry after seeing a news report about him but now more and more people's faces are getting stuck—all except Tokyo Lipscomb's face. So she holds the key. Then all hell breaks loose.

HOIST ON HER OWN PETARD

Tokyo Lipscomb, a third-year student at Penn who is athletic but also somewhat of a nerd, is mistaken for her "perfect" identical twin when her identical twin dies suddenly. So Tokyo Lipscomb seizes the chance to masquerade as her "perfect" identical twin. But when she falls in love with her identical twin's next door neighbor, a burned out ex-ballplayer named George Henry, Tokyo Lipscomb gets hoist on her own petard. Then all hell breaks loose.

I TOAD YOU SO

Tokyo Lipscomb, a third-year student at Penn, finds a toad during her morning run around the campus. When she kisses the toad it turns into George Henry, a washed-up ex-ballplayer. Then all hell breaks loose.

IN AND OUT OF THE MONEY

Tokyo Lipscomb, a third-year student at Penn, learns that her rich uncle has died and bequeathed his fortune to her—but only if she agrees to have dinner with George Henry, a washed-up ex-ballplayer. It seems simple enough but Tokyo Lipscomb falls for George Henry and when the dust settles they've both been transported back to prehistoric times. They have to get back to modern times using only their cell phones. Then all hell breaks loose.

GROUNDHOG NIGHT

Tokyo Lipscomb, a third-year student at Penn, gets a fatal illness and joins a support group where she meets a washed-up ex-ballplayer named George Henry. Their sex life is hot at first because they're facing their mortality but gradually it deteriorates into monotony until George Henry actually dies. But somehow they start having great sex again. Or is Tokyo Lipscomb just imagining it? Then all hell breaks loose.

MY FATHER, THE DEVIL

Tokyo Lipscomb, a third-year student at Penn, comes home for summer vacation and her father throws out her math books because he says numbers are tools of the devil. But then, by using math, Tokyo Lipscomb figures out that her "father" actually is the devil and her real father is George Henry, a washed-up ex-ballplayer. Then all hell breaks loose.

MAIL ORDER ALLIGATOR

An army of alligators comes out of the sewers, which is explained by a flashback to 1959. People could send away for live baby alligators advertised on the back of comic books, but then they flushed the alligators down their toilets and the alligators multiplied. Back to the present: at the last moment the army of alligators is stopped in its tracks by a humane method discovered by the unlikely couple of Tokyo Lipscomb, a third-year student at Penn, and George Henry, a washed-up ex-ballplayer. Then all hell breaks loose.

THE GRAIL GIRLS

Tokyo Lipscomb, a third-year student at Penn, gets permission to do a special field work project for an anthropology class where she and two other girls go to the Colorado Mountains in search of a ghost town that vanished off the face of the earth during a gold rush 150 years ago. George Henry, a washed-up ex-ballplayer, becomes their guide, but instead of finding the town and its gold they find the Holy Grail. Then all hell breaks loose.

BABE IN THE WOODS

Tokyo Lipscomb, a third-year student at Penn, can't get rid of a bee hive outside the window of her dorm room. We see her Google "bees" and "bee hives" but she gets nowhere until she meets George Henry, a washed-up ex-ballplayer. He is a bee expert like the guy in Jaws who was a shark expert. Then all hell breaks loose.

SHUT YOUR TRAP DOOR

Tokyo Lipscomb, a third-year student at Penn, finds the perfect off-campus apartment. But she begins to lose her grip on reality when she finds herself battling the building's ghosts. Then she puts her trust in George Henry, a washed-up ex-ballplayer who talks her into building a trap door—but the door connects to the netherworld. Then all hell breaks loose.

SORRY, RIGHT NUMBER

Tokyo Lipscomb, a third-year student at Penn, mistakenly dials the wrong number on her cell phone and finds herself involved with a subculture with a trail that leads all the way to the White House. Then the President's cell phone explodes. Fortunately he was not talking on it at the time, but he had just been talking to George Henry, a washed-up ex-ballplayer. Then all hell breaks loose.

THE GRADUATE

George Henry is a washed-up ex-ballplayer now working as an assistant baseball coach at the University of Pennsylvania. When he meets Tokyo Lipscomb, a third-year student at Penn, it comes out that George Henry never learned to read and is embarrassed about it. Then there are montages of George Henry and Tokyo Lipscomb making love intercut with scenes of George Henry learning to read. At first he's reading children's books, then young adult, and finally *Ulysses*. Meanwhile their lovemaking is also growing more elaborate. Finally we see him graduating from college. Then all hell breaks loose.

2012

Resolution and Independence

There can be no biography of him,
Who was no one and everyone
And went by many names such as
Leroy Everybodytalksabout and
Pan Smolarek and the man who
Casts no shadow. He never married
And his companion was a chicken.

Winter and summer, rain or shine,
His home was a bench in Lincoln Park
Near the old miniature golf course
Where he and the chicken performed
Loosely choreographed dumb shows.
When the police arrested him he laughed
And said, "Mene mene tekel upharsin."

He rode city bus lines with the chicken.
He carried a toy bow and arrow set.
He wore an alarm clock around his neck.
When the horseplayers gathered at night
Outside the Commonwealth Hotel
And a truck brought the *Racing Forms*,
He and the chicken were also there.

He had some literature, in Johnson's phrase,
And held Wordsworth in high regard.
The Old Leech Gatherer was a personage
To whom he often alluded—but when stung
By looks of stupefaction among his listeners
He would quote Hamlet, albeit imperfectly:
"This was caviar to the general population."

He never made any money but he was
A great businessman and was a great lover
Though he remained a virgin all his life.
"There are just so many fat people now."
Those were his last words, whose truth
I reflect upon whenever I go into Starbucks
So I try to make my own coffee at home.

2012

Al Farber Who Art in Heaven

In days of yore when the men played pinochle
At Julius Jaffe's apartment a tradition grew up,
A rhetorical set piece evolved whereby
Al Farber in manly tones would describe
The route he'd driven in his Oldsmobile
From Skokie to the Jaffe residence on
Wellington Avenue. As a rule he took
Dempster Street to Ridge Road,
To Peterson, then south on the Outer Drive
Exiting at Belmont. But oh there were occasions
When the rain fell or the snow fell or in summer's
Blaze the asphalt on Peterson Avenue buckled,
Or the Outer Drive itself was closed for some
Cockamamie reason. Then drawing himself
To his full height and waving his arms about,
Al Farber would declare, "I stayed on Dempster
All the way to Sheridan Road! I had no choice!"
Railing on and on until—falling silent as
Julius Jaffe shuffled the cards—he had the air
Of a man staring into the void. But this lasted
Only a moment, and once again he exploded
And the window panes rattled and the
Ashtrays lurched around on the card table.
"What else could I do?" he pleaded, existentially.
"Ridge Road was closed off. Traffic was a mess."

Forty years he's gone! Christ, there was a man
Who owned dozens of businesses: dump
Trucks, a line of hair care products, a bowling
Paraphernalia store, carpet cleaning equipment,
Children's furniture, sick room supplies—
All under the aegis of Al Farber Enterprises.
Yet he never ate his heart out over money
Nor in all those years we met at the Belden
Corned Beef Center did he show any interest
In financial vicissitudes. We spoke instead
Of getting from one place to another, alternate
Routes when Lincoln Avenue was congested
Or Pratt Avenue was impassable, as it often was.
In fact, the ever-worsening congestion on Pratt
And in Rogers Park as a whole caused Al Farber
To make a solemn vow. "I will no longer eat at
Ashkenaz," he told me, referring to the delicatessen
located at Pratt and Greenview. "It's not worth my
Time to sit behind the wheel for forty-five minutes
For a corned beef sandwich, especially when
A better sandwich with more meat on it can be had
At the Corned Beef Center. It isn't called
The Corned Beef Center for nothing! Aw haw
Haw haw! Ah ha ha! Aw haw haw haw haw!"

But then came the day—this too in the
Belden Corned Beef Center—when
Al Farber suddenly inclined himself

Across the Formica and spoke *sotto voce*:
"There was a time," he said, "when the
Four of us—myself, Julius Jaffe, Gus Golding,
And Charlie Shapiro—would jump in the
Car after the pinochle game and drive
To Wilmette for an ice cream cone!
There was no traffic to speak of, Mitchell.
At the most, twenty-five minutes straight up
Sheridan Road where there was a place
Called the Dairy Bar on the border of
Wilmette and Kenilworth in that unincorporated
Area referred to as No Man's Land."
Pausing abruptly, he was overcome by a
Coughing fit and turned a bright blue, but
Somehow managed to say, "In Wilmette
Jews could live, but there was not one Jew
In Kenilworth. Not one!" And he died.

Now in Los Angeles, lo, I am master of
Little-known routes and side streets bypassing
The cement mixers and FedEx trucks parked
On LaBrea Avenue or Highland. What others
Take forty minutes to drive, I can drive in twenty.
But this too is vanity because—and I make this
Public for the first time—I always feel not lost
Exactly, but not really *there*. Turning left
From Wilshire onto Rimpau, inwardly I head
North on Crawford Avenue in Lincolnwood,

Passing the Bryn Mawr Country Club, skirting
The sewage treatment plant at Howard Street,
On and on, all the way to Wilmette Avenue
Where Crawford becomes Hunter Road.
Picking up the children at Franklin and Western,
What in my mind's eye do I see but the electric
blue roof light of a Chicago police car weaving
In and out of traffic on Milwaukee Avenue near
Where the Como Inn was. But the worst or best
Is this: alone in the Passat, I'm with Al Farber
In the Oldsmobile the day he thought the hell with it
And stayed on Foster Avenue all the way
To Nagle. "I'm staying on Foster!" he cried,
And struck the steering wheel to challenge God.
But bear with my muse. It is not as it was.

2009

Mr. Tivy

Mr. Tivy was able to talk with animals, or even birds, and he believed a successful film could be made about his ability: In the film he would receive profitable tips from a thoroughbred racehorse. It was a farfetched story. In real life horses were as fatuous about handicapping as Mr. Tivy himself, which he had discovered by listening to several of the beasts. But what a movie it would make. The public would pay money to see it.

Mondays and Tuesdays were Mr. Tivy's nights off. One Monday he was well cared-for in a massage parlor on North Clark Street. Later, back in his room, he savored the memory as he stared at the ceiling or watched television. When he fell asleep it came to him in a dream that if he pinched his pennies for seven nights he could stride back into the Sultan's Palace with the means to really enjoy himself. But he was weak. Tuesday night he told Brownie, "I'm going out."

"It's up to you," came the reply from beneath the bed as the door closed behind Mr. Tivy.

At the Palace he placed twenty on the counter and requested Gwill. Gwill remembered him, smiled, and led him by his good hand toward a cubicle.

"What's the matter with your other hand, anyway, Dave?" she inquired, wrinkling up her nose, as they passed through a curtain of beads hanging in the doorway.

"Arthritis," Mr. Tivy explained.

"But you're so young!"

"Forty-six!" As Gwill washed her own hands in a basin attached to the wall he added, "Actually, it can hit you at any age, arthritis can."

But now the time for conversation was past. With a sigh Gwill turned off the faucet and approached the medical examining table on which Mr. Tivy had eagerly taken a seat. As she manipulated him—this was what twenty dollars could buy—he lay back and really enjoyed the way she went about it compared to other massage-parlor girls. He studied Gwill through half-closed eyes. Her pink housecoat hung open. Were he and this woman meant for each other? Suddenly he powerfully ejaculated. There was a loud meow. Lolling his head to the left, Mr. Tivy saw that the Sultan's Palace mascot had wandered into the cubicle. He decided to make the most of this.

When he'd caught his breath, he announced, "Gwill, I'm going to tell you a secret."

Gwill was washing up again. "What's that?" she idly asked.

"Something I've never told anybody," he lied. He was always telling everybody.

"Okay, okay." But by the second okay she meant, *make this up to me in your tip.*

Sliding off the examining table, Mr. Tivy zipped up his pants. He placed his good hand on Gwill's shoulder and said, "You see that cat?" With his gnarled left hand he indicated the animal, which sat with its tail curled around its legs. The tip twitched enigmatically.

"That's Gross Out," Gwill explained. Mr. Tivy squeezed her shoulder and knelt beside the creature.

"Come on!" he cajoled. "It's time, it's time! They'll make it into a movie! Let's show her what we can do! Say something!"

But when, after a moment, the cat only blinked, he snarled, "Why, you..."

Mr. Tivy swung at Gross Out, who hissed, darted under the examining table, and sat down again. Now the frustrated show-off heard laughter behind him. He turned and saw Gwill's face reddening. She giggled uncontrollably as she would always giggle, whenever she repeated this story, in all the massage parlors she would work in, to all the girls who thought they'd seen everything. Mr. Tivy's stricken look made the whole thing funnier. Suddenly she dashed through the bead curtain to describe this guy to whatever girls were free.

Still on his knees, Mr. Tivy stared after her. He had loved Gwill. "You're being silly," the cat said, as if reading his thoughts.

Mr. Tivy shot back a killing look. "I wanted to be somebody in her eyes!" He reflected a moment, then demanded, "What'd you meow for?"

"Hungry."

"I thought you wanted to help me out."

"You know what you're asking can never be."

"But..."

"Besides," interrupted the feline, "if I was going to talk, I would have just talked..."

Mr. Tivy's head drooped. His jaw hung open an inch.

"...and anyway, what is she but a lowlife broad wasting her time in dives? On the other hand, you're a remarkable person! A precious gift was given to you. Go to Lincoln Park and spend some time at the large-mammal house! Gain the wisdom of the elephants!"

Mr. Tivy had heard all this before. "You talk like my dog," he bitterly mused. Just then laughter was heard from the hall. The cat's eyes went blank. Mr. Tivy got to his feet as several girls rushed into the cubicle, together with an enormous Mexican bouncer.

A few moments later, the door of the Sultan's Palace slammed shut behind Mr. Tivy.

It was winter. Tiny ice crystals whipped through the night air. The disappointed man squinted down Clark Street toward the looming IBM building, the Sears Tower with its flashing strobe light, and the John Hancock Center. So this was how, for another week, his night off would end. He made his way toward State Street to wait for the number thirty-six bus, and a long wait it proved to be.

Setting his collar against the wind, Mr. Tivy stood under a lamppost as passing automobiles sprayed snow at his feet. At last the bus arrived.

Mr. Tivy climbed out of the darkness into the brightly lit vehicle, deposited his fare in the box with a clang, and declared to the ragtag assembly of passengers, "I talk to animals and they talk to me! They speak perfect English. You name it, I've had a conversation with it. I'm the only one they'll talk to. Don't ask me why, I'm not a scientist. I grew up on the far South Side. We were poor. I didn't like to play with the other kids although my hand was okay then. Look at it now! One night when I was six years old a rat wakes me up and says, 'Davy, your mother wants you to know she's very proud of you.' I thought something was wrong so I says, 'What's going on?' and the rat says, 'She just now passed away in the other room.' That's how poor we were! I found out my mother died from a rat!"

Weak smiles on the faces of the male passengers greeted this diatribe, while the women—they were nurses and office cleaners—remained impassive. The riders of the late-night buses were inured to crazy people. There was the guy with the big alarm clock, for instance, and the man who passed out paper napkins. Now here was the man who talked to animals. A few of the travelers had even heard Mr. Tivy before.

He continued, "I'll never forget when, years ago, a duck..."

"Mister, take a seat," interrupted the driver.

Abruptly silent, Mr. Tivy slumped onto a molded plastic bench. His mouth was set in a tight line. He resolved to say nothing for the rest of the ride.

1983

"To no place he is called..."

To no place he is called
And thither he is bound—
Cloudbursts, desiccated plains,
Nothing slows his Volkswagen.
Old Philadelphia disappears
In the trembling rearview mirror,
Chicago looms, then vanishes,
Houston fades, Dallas evanesces.
Those years of the yearning siren
Voice's call—the longing intonation
Unheard or unacknowledged—
They like the towns and cities lie
Behind him now as to no place
He is called and thither he is bound.

2010

"Do not be a gentleman when you say goodnight..."

Do not be a gentleman when you say goodnight,
Nor let silence prevail at the closing of the door;
Hit him with your left, then hit him with your right.

Myron Fox played pinochle though had lost his sight,
With hand and heart discerning cards' worth;
Do not be a gentleman when you say goodnight.

Jess Rabin cheekily liked to say go fly a kite,
A turn of phrase we don't hear any more;
Hit him with your left, then hit him with your right.

Al Arenberg got rich with a non-glare ceiling light,
He died in a room of the old Webster Hotel;
Do not be a gentleman when you say goodnight.

Dark as the nights were, so the windows were bright,
The boys and their girlfriends on the dance floor;
Hit him with your left, then hit him with your right.

Lou Belmont! I see him now with my own second sight,
The black Oldsmobile—and the stern ukase:
'Do not be a gentleman when you say goodnight,
'Hit him with your left, then hit him with your right.'

2014

The Death of Molesworth

The dog Grandpa Munster was loved and respected by Molesworth.

In 1974, the dog died in battle and Molesworth got him stuffed. He stood proudly beside Molesworth's TV set.

Molesworth himself died on the day of the Super Bowl game, 1977.

In the months leading up to that day, I was working for Molesworth as handy man, official representative, and bet placer at dog matches. Molesworth did not own dogs during the period of my employment, nor did he venture from his home anymore to attend dog matches in person. However, he knew all the dog men and dog activity in the Texas-Louisiana area, and he never lost a bet that he told me to place.

On account of the cancer eating away at his liver, Molesworth had a small machine strapped on his side. It pumped medicine into the affected organ. It ticked like a clock, counting off his remaining hours, minutes, and seconds on Earth!

Molesworth was not able to do his wife. Compared to him, she was young, my age, in fact, named Suzan, with a z.

We petted, frenched, et cetera, but that was all, on account of my code of morality.

★

On the night before the 1977 Super Bowl game, Molesworth obtained an old boar badger from a guy that had caught it.

The next morning he said, "Let's have some fun on this day of the Super Bowl."

He called McGhee on the telephone and he said, "McGhee, drive on over and we will watch the football game. And if you would like a chance to take some of my money, bring that forty-five pound male you think so highly of."

He hung up and he told Suzan, "Go into the bedroom, Suzan, get some hundreds, stuff them into your bra."

Which she did.

Molesworth, Suzan, and I sat in the back yard awaiting McGhee. The badger was under a turned-over oil drum.

By and by McGhee walked into the yard, his dog remaining out in his truck.

Beers were drunk.

McGhee said, "Molesworth, what is this proposition you got me over here for? I know it wasn't to watch no football game."

Molesworth pointed at the oil drum and revealed that it contained a badger. He continued:

"The drum will be tipped on its side. Your dog gets one minute to pull him out of there. Simple as that."

"For how much?"

"Two hundred."

"Five hundred!"

"Let me see your money."

"Ha, ha, you old peckerwood," McGhee laughed while he pulled out his roll.

Meanwhile, Suzan and I had merely observed these goings on as innocent bystanders. Now Molesworth declared, "My money's stuffed down her bra for good luck. Show him, darling."

Whereupon Suzan pulled out the money.

McGhee grinned like a fool at the sight of it. He handed Suzan his own money, told her to put it right where Molesworth's was.

He then went off to get his pit bull, named Monster Man.

About a year and a half old, with a reputation as a hard-biting dog, the dog Monster Man had won two fights.

Entering the back yard, he pulled at his chain as the smell of the badger met his nose.

McGhee jerked back on the chain, said, "Let's start the fracas, my dog wants to bite something!"

Molesworth: "Now hold on. Who's going to be the timekeeper?"

McGhee: "I don't give a shit. Let Neff keep time."

I said, "I don't have a watch or nothing."

Molesworth: "That's all right, son. Just count up to sixty like this. One Mississippi, two Mississippi."

McGhee: "I can't hold this bulldog!"

I turned the drum over. As the dog Monster Man entered it, I started to count. The fracas progressed and the drum began to roll around, so Molesworth told me to sit astraddle of it.

Which I did and kept on counting.

Then, "Sixty Mississippi."

The badger was still in the drum.

Molesworth told me in his soft little voice, "Son, pull McGhee's dog out of there." However, McGhee himself reached in and pulled the dog out by the hind legs, staring at the animal like he was some cur.

"A badger," Molesworth patiently explained, "each and every time he bites, he twists and takes a plug out of you. A badger can be a half-bad animal. McGhee, I hope you'll stick around to watch the ball game."

But McGhee merely inquired of Molesworth, "You still got that little snubby you used to carry in your pocket?"

"Why, yes."

"Let me borrow it a second."

Whereupon the older man handed it over, whereupon McGhee reached down and shot the dog Monster Man in the back of the head, whereupon he tossed the snubby back to Molesworth and departed the back yard and we heard his truck starting up.

Molesworth just laughed. "Grandpa Munster, why, one time he had a badger out of the drum and stone dead in fifty seconds."

Suzan spoke up: "Can I have the five hundred?"

But Molesworth only stood up and shuffled off toward the house.

So it seemed like, as he often did, he was choosing to ignore her words.

Except then he said, "Keep the five hundred, you whore." Said it just as the door slammed behind him.

Whereupon Suzan told me: "I hate that old man. He is my husband in name only. I got an idea, Neff, been thinking about it a good long time. Let's knock him over the head, take all his money, steal his car, drive about three hundred miles, fuck all night, and just leave him your old truck to remember us by."

When I chose not to give her the courtesy of a reply, she went inside. I burned the carcass of Monster Man in a garbage pail. Next, taking the badger out of the oil drum, I saw that it was bit up, and it soon died of its own accord. Whereupon I burned it, too, in the garbage pail. It was eleven o'clock in the morning, but it seemed like a lot of time had gone by.

⋆

Pretty soon the afternoon rolled around and it was getting close to the time for the 1977 Super Bowl, Oakland Raiders versus Minnesota Vikings.

With Molesworth in the comfort of his reclining chair, we were in the living room watching the pregame festivities on TV. Watching as usual with the sound turned off, for Molesworth disliked all the announcers. Each and every one of them was a Citizen Joe!

Suzan was sitting on the sofa, legs crossed in her typical fashion, and sitting on the other sofa was me.

Quite suddenly Molesworth kind of lolled his head in my direction and said, "Neff, you want to bet on the Super Bowl game?"

"No thank you."

"Neff, you got to bet on the Super Bowl game. I'll bet you five thousand dollars against your old truck. Suzan, go in the bedroom and get five thousand dollars."

"Hey, I'm not going to bet with you."

"Oh, all right. You cur out. You suck eggs. You are a cake eater."

Lolling his head back around towards the TV screen, Molesworth wheezed his famous cackle laugh as the kickoff floated through the air of whatever stadium they were playing in. Then he stopped laughing.

Whereupon it was quiet for a good long while, no sound on the TV.

Whereupon Molesworth said, "Neff, come here and put your hands under my ass."

I saw that Molesworth's eyes had revolved back into his head. I stood up. Suzan stood up. We were looking at Molesworth, whereupon his eyes came back to normal.

He said: "Neff, come here, get down on your knees and put your hands under my ass."

I thought to myself, this is the last request of a dying old man, so you better obey it.

His ass was just skin and bone.

He said, "Neff, years ago I had a vasectomy. The reason was, I was doing so many women that I was afraid one of them was going to charge me with a paternity suit. Later on though I started wanting something I never cared about before, an offspring where I could pass on my bulldog knowledge, learned over the course of a lifetime. Dr. Mulligan, who had performed the original operation, he told me, 'What I did, I can undo.' But then I got to thinking, got to worrying how old I'd be till the child was grown, whereupon I got the cancer anyhow. Meanwhile, I decided to hire you, Neff, in order to pass on to you all this priceless knowledge of the American pit bull terrier. Yes, I did manage to pass on some of the knowledge, for which I'm glad. Because I have been having this funny feeling about not living past the Super Bowl game, and now I realize that I am truly not going to live past it."

"Should I call the hospital? Should I call the ambulance?" I asked.

"No, goddammit! Neff, I got a shitload of money and South African Krugerrands squirreled away here in the house, plus my valuable collection of old-time dogfight movies. I want you to have everything, Neff. Everything is yours! I have already given you my most valuable possession, my bulldog knowledge, so I want you to have everything else too. Don't spend good money on my funeral. Just plant me in the back yard, where so many good dogs took their shits over the years, or better yet burn me up like that pit dog this morning, or like that old badger."

So the last word of Molesworth's life was *badger.* He closed his eyes. I pulled out my hands. Suzan shut off the TV set, and I knew she was pissed.

Royally pissed, because Molesworth's entire farewell speech was directed to me! Suzan did not get so much as a single good-bye!

Suzan: "Well, fuck me! It makes me sick to think of all the times I swabbed his yellow body with smelly alcohol! Anyway, he's gone, flew the coop. By the way, Neff, just in case you got any ideas, every single thing he owned legally belongs to me, his lawfully wedded wife."

To which I had this to say: "Suzan, you are a totally materialistic person. No one will deny you've got a great body, but battery acid flows in your veins. You go right ahead and help yourself to the shoeboxes full of money and all the Krugerrands! I'll just take the dogfight movies, and not because of their monetary value either. However, I don't expect you to understand that, Suzan."

Whereupon she directed at me the stare of a woman totally inflamed by pure hatred.

"I am taking the dogfight movies and I am gonna drop 'em into a dumpster someplace."

"You are not taking 'em."

"I AM TAKING 'EM, AND IF YOU TRY TO STOP ME, IF YOU TRY TO TOUCH ME, ASSHOLE, I'LL FUCKING KILL YOU!"

Whereupon she went looking for the snubby...

Went looking through Molesworth's pockets for it...

However, the snubby was nowhere to be found!

Yes, it seemed that, even in death, Molesworth was one jump ahead of the rest of everybody. Result: Suzan was one hundred percent frustrated and totally wet hen mad at the world.

Throwing Molesworth's body onto the floor like a sack of potatoes, she declared: "To that old man, I was just something he could show off to his 'neck pals like one of their prize bulldogs. Used me, that's what Molesworth did! And Neff, you have also hurt my feelings real bad. You rejected me, and you were a hypocrite, the way you would do everything with me but fuck me. Then, out there in the back yard, when I said let's take a chance and run away, you got up on your high horse! Oh, fuck ass, shit ass, fuck!"

Whereupon she wound up to take a kick at Molesworth's corpse. Wound up to take a good kick at it, just like in the Super Bowl game.

Whereupon I shoved her backwards, trying to do her a favor actually, for I knew such a kick would haunt her the rest of her days.

But she still wanted to kick something. Had to kick something, as a matter of fact. Whereupon her eyes lit on Grandpa Munster, his stuffed self, and this is what she kicked.

Grandpa Munster fell over, and the snubby was lying on the carpet, there in the faded patch where the platform used to be!

Why had Molesworth, for what twisted reason in his brain, why had he hidden the snubby under the dog? He was sure one of a kind.

Suzan grabbed the snubby, aimed it right at me. She said, "Neff, want to hear something really wild? This very second we could have been in a Holiday Inn someplace, fucking. But I never fucked a man I wouldn't rather shoot."

Whereupon she pulled the trigger.

People are always curious what it feels like. Doesn't hurt at first, but gradually the blood fills up in the bullet hole till it spills on over, like a full tank of gas. It's something I remember whenever I fill up my truck.

Also, the shot might not knock you over, but pretty soon you get too weak to stand up.

Lying there on the floor, I was miserable. Suzan was gone. Now there was just the three of us, Molesworth, Grandpa Munster, and I, two of us dead and one of us working on it. But I made an effort not to get all down in the dumps.

Yes, I thought about the bulldogs I'd seen hurt worse. Seen them hurt ten times worse! Seen them get up and almost come back from the dead!

Whereupon I saw a man come walking into the room. I recognized this man. It was Ben Cartwright from *Bonanza*, which had been one of Molesworth's favorite shows. Mine too.

Ben Cartwright got down on the floor beside me and held my hand. He said, "Vietnam, Watergate, lines of cars at the gas pumps, gun control laws, women's liberation, so-called animal lovers, drug addicts, welfare cheats, the fifty-five mile per hour speed limit. These are hard times. The country is sick, and it's going to get worse before it gets better. The same is true of you, Neff, because you are a metaphor for America. But here's the good news. Just as your wounds are going to heal, the United States is going to grow strong again. When? Soon. How? Well, I want you to picture a good-humored man with nothing chickenshit about him. He is not fat. He likes to dress in a plaid work shirt, Levis, and cowboy boots. He likes to begin the day with orange juice, bacon and eggs, and coffee, and he likes to end the day with steak, a baked potato, pie a la mode, a nightcap, bed with his wife. Who is this man? You will know his name. The whole country will know his name!"

Whereupon Ben Cartwright was gone.

That was in 1977. At first, I wondered at his meaning, even wondered if he had really existed at all! In 1980, I thought he was talking about Ronald Reagan. Now, I just don't know.

1986

Duke Rhino

Some say your name
Is your destiny as with
Green Bay's Bart Starr
Who became the star QB
Of the Lombardi teams
Or Dick Butkus who cussed
And butted his way
To football immortality.

Joe Montana was another
Great QB whose name conjured
Images of Old West gunslingers
Or 19th-century riverboat gamblers
And that day in the park when
I first came across his name
In the *Tribune* I knew Joe Montana
Would be in the Hall of Fame.

But what about Jim Brown?
Possibly the top ball carrier
Of all time who (oddly?)
Played for the Cleveland Browns
Yet it's hard to come up
With a blander, less dashing,

More forgettable or invisible
Name than Jim Brown.

Earl Scheib too bore the burden
Of a genuinely *zhlubby* name
Yet he built a multi-million dollar
Automobile painting and collision
Repair company with locations
Around the world for which Scheib
Even made the paint though it
All did go to hell eventually.

My own name was Donald G. Bruce
But only for one day until my black
Market adoption took place and
This present appellation was conferred
On me but now as shadows lengthen
On the greensward and evening
Draws nigh I shall henceforth and
Forever be known as Duke Rhino!

2013

Goomniak to Freed

His family name was Goomniak but at fifty he changed it to Freed. Why Freed? Because he was *freed* of the name Goomniak. As a child he had been laughed at for his name, and even as an adult he had been aware of suppressed laughter.

When he became Freed his business took off. His company sold mail-order costume jewelry. His niche was Army and Navy enlisted personnel whom he reached through ads in military newspapers and magazines.

Now, with his new name, Freed began an internet marketing campaign on military websites. It was like striking oil. Orders doubled at first, then tripled.

One online ad showed a lady's gold-plated ring mounted with a tiny diamond. The price was a hundred dollars. But a red line ran through the price, with text below: "Pay just $50 if you're in the military!"

More text: "Order by the Fourth of July and pay only $40!"

Then: "Include this code word with your order and subtract another ten percent! The code word is BUTTERCUP."

Finally, in bold italics: ***"You risk nothing! Full money back guarantee!"***

Since the rings cost Freed only three dollars, his business was like a cash machine. The more money he made, the better he felt. He was introducing himself as Jerome Freed or Jerry Freed, and no one was laughing at him anymore.

He divorced his wife. He *freed* himself of her. The cost was high but so what? Their children were grown and his wife had become a millstone around his neck. A millstone was something heavy and Biblical.

With his new confidence and his improved income Freed was attractive to women. His sex life took off like his business. He would never get married again. "Not in a million years," he told his friends. "I'm having too much fun."

One night, lying in bed with a beautiful woman asleep beside him, Freed reflected on the self-sabotaging tendency that had afflicted him for so many years. Why had he remained Goomniak? At any moment he could have become Freed.

Freed drifted off to sleep, and in that same hour he dreamed that he was locking the front door of his apartment. As he secured the lock and felt the bolt go out, the door somehow opened and a well-dressed businessman rushed past him. Freed awoke in terror.

★

Friends since childhood, Freed and Mel Patak met weekly for lunch at a cafeteria in the jewelry district. Amid the clattering of knives and forks they amused and needled each other.

But on the day after Freed's dream, Mel Patak saw that something was wrong. "Jerry, are you okay?" he asked.

Freed said, "I'm going to die. I don't know where and I don't know how. But I will die very soon."

Mel stared across the table. "Are you sick? Have you seen a doctor?"

"A doctor won't help," Freed said. He told Mel about his dream of the locked door opening and the well-dressed businessman. The dream predicted his imminent death.

Mel saw this was not a joke. Freed's face was pale. He looked like he could die there in the cafeteria. Mel said, "Jerry, have you ever heard of Rabbi Michael Mushnik?"

"No," Freed answered, "I've never heard of him."

Mel took his cellphone from his pocket. He said, "You need to see Rabbi Michael Mushnik about your dream. It's probably nothing, but you need to see Rabbi Michael Mushnik." Mel punched a message into the phone as Freed watched skeptically.

A moment passed. Mel was staring at the phone. Then he brightened. He lit up like an electric sign. "Yes! Rabbi Michael Mushnik will see you immediately!" He took a pen from his shirt pocket, scribbled an address on a napkin, and slid it across the table to Freed.

Freed glanced at the address. It was not far away, but he was reluctant. After all, what was the use? "I'll have to close the office," he said.

"Close it then!" Mel's voice was rising. "Close the office!"

Freed shrugged. "Okay, Mel, take it easy."

"Good." Mel looked relieved. "Go right now. And Jerry, bring some money."

★

The address was a brick warehouse converted to trendy living spaces. Could this be a home for a rabbi? On a directory beside the entrance Freed pushed the "Mushnik" button. He was buzzed in at once.

He entered a brightly lit foyer. At the far end was an elevator and, to one side, a sharply inclined stairway. A voice came from above: "Hi! Just take the stairs! I'm one flight up!"

Freed climbed the stairway. On the second floor landing a large young man appeared. Freed recognized the uniform of an observant Jew: white shirt, black trousers, a knit kippah on his head. "Welcome, Jerry! I'm Rabbi Michael Mushnik!"

They shook hands. The rabbi grinned, squinting behind thick glasses. "Let's go inside." As they crossed the landing toward an open door, Freed noted the ritually knotted fringes, *tzitzit*, dangling from beneath the rabbi's untucked shirt.

"Were you *bar mitzvah*, Jerry? I'm just curious," Mushnik asked.

Freed was actually uncertain. "I think so."

"Ha ha! You think so but you don't remember for sure. Well, if you were, your name is inscribed in the Book of Life."

They entered a spacious loft—1,500 square feet, Freed estimated—cluttered with furniture, cardboard boxes, book cases, sofas, bicycles. There was a cat litter smell.

Mushnik closed the door, then spread his arms in an all-encompassing gesture. "Torah is so large, Jerry. It's not just wide, but also deep. Nobody except a *tzaddik* can understand the whole thing. My specialty is *Chaye Sarah*: 105 verses, 1,402 words, and 5,314 Hebrew letters."

Still grinning, he cocked his head to one side. "Say something, Jerry. Don't be shy."

But Freed did feel shy, or disoriented. "You're a large man," he managed to say. "I mean, you did refer to the largeness of the Torah."

"That's right!" Mushnik laughed, as if this were just what he'd been waiting to hear. He clapped Freed on the shoulder. "I wrestled at 285. Now I'm about 250. Here's my study."

His study was enclosed, walled off by bookcases, like a child's fort. On a narrow desk lay an open book of densely lettered Hebrew. "Make yourself comfortable," said the rabbi, indicating a folding chair. He sat down at the desk, turned his eyes toward the ceiling, and sighed.

"How do I have the merit to see the future? The truth is, I don't have that merit. No one does except the *tzaddikim*. But for reasons known only to himself—and I often ask myself why—Hashem has bestowed that aspect of his light upon me."

He stared at Freed, still cheerful but intense. "Mel Patak texted me about why you're here, Jerry. You're afraid you're going to die. And, unfortunately, I see you are correct. Your time is just about up. You had a dream about this, I gather?"

Freed's heart sank. He felt helpless, hopeless. "I had a nightmare," he whispered. "I was locking the door to my apartment. Then the door opened and a well-dressed businessman rushed past me. I woke up in terror."

Mushnik nodded. "The well-dressed businessman symbolizes death, obviously. But you want to live, right? So I need to know why you want to live, Jerry. Tell me why you want to live, and I'll be fully motivated to help you."

Though still shaken, Freed felt unexpected anger. Why

did he want to live? It was a ridiculous and insulting question. "Rabbi, I want to live because I don't want to die." he said. "It's natural. Life resists death."

"Yes, all life resists death," Mushnik agreed. "A cockroach resists death. A paramecium resists death. But are you a cockroach or a paramecium? Don't you have some higher purpose, Jerry? What is your *raison d'etre*?" he demanded, in awkward French.

Freed's heart was pounding. "I certainly do have a purpose," he proudly stated, and added in an accusing tone, "But I doubt you'll think it's a higher purpose. You're a rabbi, but my purpose isn't studying the Torah."

"Of course. But there are many ways of studying Torah, Jerry. In the Jewish religion the word 'study' has a multiplicity of meanings. So does the word 'Torah' for that matter. Just be completely honest with me. Lay your cards on the table. Let the chips fall where they may."

"All right, fine. My purpose in life is to make love with beautiful women. For years I ignored the women who passed through my life. My name was Goomniak. I was an upstanding citizen. But I changed my name to Freed!" he exulted.

"No kidding? Really?" Mushnik inquired. He seemed fascinated. "Your name was Goomniak, but now your name is Freed. And when you changed your name, I'll bet your life changed too. Because you're having sex more often, right?"

Freed was encouraged. "Absolutely. Beautiful women are flocking to me and we're fucking. Excuse my language. And the more of them I fuck, the more I understand the deep meaning of it. Sometimes, even during the act itself, I mentally step back and see how this is what I was born to do!"

"Wow. Just wow," said the rabbi. "What can I tell you? *Kodosh, kodosh, kodosh*, holy, holy, holy is the lord of hosts, the whole Earth is full of his glory." He thought for a moment. "Okay, here's something you'll be interested in. Here's something to think about. . . ."

He spoke in a confiding tone. "Jerry, there's a verse in *Chaye Sarah*—it reads, 'Abraham was old and stricken with years'—and that verse anticipates the opening verse of the Book of Kings, which reads, 'King David was old and stricken with years.' Do you grasp the significance of that?"

As to draw energy from the sacred letters, the rabbi placed his hands on the Hebrew book. "You see, David was the reincarnation of Abraham. That's my personal opinion. Some would disagree. Neither here nor there. Anyway . . ."

He leaned across the desk toward Freed. "King David was on his deathbed, Jerry. He was cold. The servants covered him with blankets, but he was still cold. So what did they do, Jerry?"

He slapped the desktop. The sound was like a gunshot. "They found a girl named Abishag the Shunammite. Of course, that name means nothing to you. Abishag the Shunammite? It's like a bunch of nonsense syllables. So I'd like you to do me a favor, my friend . . .

"I'd like you to imagine the hottest woman in the history of the world. Then I'd like you to imagine a woman even hotter than that. Much hotter! As we read in the Book of Daniel, 'The furnace was heated seven times hotter than ever before. . . .'

"That unbelievably hot woman was Abishag the Shunammite. Eighteen or nineteen years old. Perfect body. Beautiful long hair. Totally uninhibited. They put Abishag the Shunammite in bed with King David, to warm him up, so to speak."

He stopped. He seemed to relax. Was that the end of the story? "So what happened?" Freed asked.

"Aha!" Mushnik exploded, fully charged again. "He wants to know what happened! Well, Rav Shimon Shalom Kalish of Amshinov says one thing happened, but Rav Moshe Yitzchak Gewirtzman of Pshevorsk says something else happened!"

But abruptly, disarmingly, his tone changed again. Now he was solemn. "Did you bring any money, Jerry?"

Freed was taken aback. "Money?"

"Yes. How much money did you bring me to save you from the *malakh hamavet*, the angel of death? Five thousand dollars? Ten thousand?"

"I brought five hundred," said Freed.

The rabbi vigorously shook his head. "What! Five hundred? Did Patak tell you to bring five hundred dollars?"

"Patak didn't tell me what to bring."

Mushnik was thunderstruck. "Patak means goose in Bulgarian," he muttered.

He seemed genuinely depressed. "Well, put it here," he said, struggling to recover. "Let me see the cash." He tapped the desk. Freed took five bills from his pocket and placed them down.

Mushnik gazed sadly at the money. Looking back at Freed, he spoke slowly and emphatically, as if to an idiot: "All right, instead of you dying, Jerry, thirteen Jewish men are going to die in your place."

"Thirteen men?" Freed was incredulous.

"Jewish men," the rabbi emphasized. "But don't stress. They were going to die anyway. It's an administrative issue. I can't explain it." He waved his hand dismissively, then removed his glasses. He looked younger without them, like a teenager or even a baby.

"Now I'm going to enter a trance," he said, rubbing his eyes. "While I'm in my trance I'll recite the names of the thirteen Jewish men. Then I'll stay in the trance for a while. So please just show yourself out."

Rising slightly, he stuffed the money into his pocket. "That's all there is to it. Any questions? Everything okay?" His mood was elevating. He was becoming cheerful again, his old self.

"Um, rabbi," Freed said, "what if it doesn't work?"

But Mushnik seemed not to have heard. His eyes were already closed. His face sagged, shoulders slumped. In a voice dreamy and distant, but firm, he said, "Lou Margolis!"

It was the first name. Quiet followed. Freed waited, first confused, then impatient. Mushnik was breathing deeply. Was he asleep?

"Bernard Inlander! Stuart L. Kroll! Herman Fishman! Mort Shaeffer!"

Using his fingers, Freed tried to keep count of the names. Five so far. Meanwhile, something new and strange was happening. Freed found himself believing in this. It was a tenuous belief for the moment, like a fish tug on a line. He wanted to manage it correctly.

"Harry Perlin! Samuel Niederberger!"

Seven names. Another, longer hiatus began, but Freed felt confident. He had seen it happen before.

"Leo Klein! Marshall Moscowitz!"

Nine names. Freed was really feeling much better. Giddy, in fact. Now he understood Mushnik's indignation about the five hundred dollars. It was indeed far too little to pay. But five million would also be too little, because you can't put a price tag on life.

"Norman Wilner!"

The rabbi's breaths were becoming shorter. His face was turning red, his eyes were closed tight. Freed closed his own eyes. The possibility of becoming more observant of his religion occurred to him. Did God exist?

"Eli Aptaker!

Two names to go.

"Chester Shultz!"

Freed opened his eyes. He looked at his hands. He'd counted twelve names. Just one more....

"Abe Nosek!"

That was it. A wave of warm emotion engulfed Freed. Behind the desk, Mushnik now had a serene look, as if he'd given birth. His breathing was steady, his chin was resting on his chest. Freed realized that Mushnik was a good man, a decent man.

He wanted to hug and kiss Mushnik. He would never forget Mushnik. Nothing was now as important to Freed as not waking Mushnik. He would show himself out the door, as Mushnik had said. He would let the good man peacefully repose.

On tiptoe at first, and then padding quietly along, Freed made his way past the rabbi and out of the loft.

★

Darkness had fallen. As he flagged a taxi, Freed felt the city's night energy rising. He felt himself reborn. He felt himself redeemed. He would celebrate with a sexual adventure, something he'd often thought about. He would have sex with two women at the same time.

In the taxi he consulted a list of women on his phone and chose two: Ellen and Evelyn. He had no doubt they'd agree to participate. For one thing—and he was frank with himself about this—he always compensated a woman for her time as they kissed goodbye.

Ellen: she worked in a men's sportswear shop, honing her skills of flattery and flirtation. Freed knew that most of what she said to him was garbage, but sexually she was so ardent and authentic that her screams of pleasure sometimes alarmed him.

Evelyn: she was from the Russian city of Ufa and had a humdrum job in a fitness club. Yet Evelyn held a mysterious allure for Freed, who had grown up before the fall of the Soviet Union. Once, lying on top of Evelyn, he realized that she was a sort of forbidden fruit and started fucking her with renewed energy.

Back in his apartment, visions of the coming hours disclosed themselves to Freed with perfect clarity. Delightfully lewd snapshots of what was going to happen flashed in his imagination as he began sending text messages to Ellen and Evelyn. During his marriage—all those years—a threesome with hot young women would have been unimaginable. Even one day ago, when he was under a sentence of death, simply waking up alive in the morning seemed too much to hope for.

As he knew they would be, Ellen and Evelyn were free that evening. As he expected, they were eager for the adventure he proposed. They were coming right over. They couldn't wait. None of this surprised Freed. He set up some candles in his bedroom.

What did surprise him, what took his breath away, was how far the threesome exceeded his wildest dreams. Ellen and Evelyn had never met before. They claimed to be "same sex virgins." Yet they tore off their clothes and rushed at each other as if magnetized.

Freed watched, wild-eyed, comparing their asses and breasts. Then, interposing himself between the two women on the bed, he began arranging them on top of himself and on top of each other in every configuration he could possibly think of.

There was no limit to this, none whatsoever. The sexual possibilities were expanding like the universe itself. Could it ever end? But then, standing beside the bed during a momentary interlude, Evelyn suddenly launched herself into the air like a leaping sailfish, executed a front flip, and landed on her back on the mattress.

There was a split second of stunned silence, then uncontrollable laughter. Freed had never laughed so hard in his life. As he and Ellen struggled to catch their breath, Evelyn explained that as a child in Ufa she had practiced gymnastics. More laughter ensued.

But the mood was slowly changing. In the glow of the guttering candles quiet talk evolved, then whispers, then silence. Ellen and Evelyn were asleep. Ellen was beside Freed, with Evelyn beyond. Resting on his side, Freed was able to loll one of his legs over both their asses at once.

Here again, as in Rabbi Mushnik's study area, Freed was awake amid the sleep of others. And now he felt for these dear women the same unaccustomed magnanimity he'd felt for the rabbi. He must let Ellen and Evelyn sleep, as he'd let Rabbi Mushnik sleep. He could wake them later and fuck again. He was beginning to feel sleepy himself.

Who would have believed it? Life could seem predictable but it was actually unpredictable. He had assumed he would always be Goomniak. Some self-sabotaging tendency had caused him to think so. But he became Freed.

His business had been stagnant, but it became a money machine. His sex life had been nonexistent, but now beautiful women were flocking to him. The dream of the well-dressed businessman had seemed to portend his doom, but Rabbi Mushnik had appeared. Freed drifted off to sleep, and in that same hour he died.

2015

Balzac Speaks of Salvation Through Sexual Intercourse

How else to keep alive the spirit
Of *sans souci*, the flame of youth,
But with sexual intercourse?
That sphere of glowing delight
To which, once I acceded to it,
The luminous channel has never
Closed to me—as all my work
Is wrought there, charity obliges
That I advertise its pleasures and
Fairly attribute the curious vitality
Derived there that each night
Invents names and faces for me
As if my heart were still a boy's
And my pen were the prick of one.

2014

The Devotions of Jean Blysema

My whole point in writing this is to tell the story of what's been happening to me and at the same time to put down some of the prayers I use to make it that much easier.

What is the meaning of life? Most people are too busy with their everyday affairs to think about this question. But now and then an ordinary housewife has time to sit down with a cup of coffee and philosophize. Since I am an ordinary housewife and since we have no children I am at home alone most of the day.

I have concluded that the meaning of life is simply to try to make one other person happy during each 24-hour period. It can be the same person for several periods or it can be different people. This is the realization I have arrived at. True, we are not going to change the world this way, but it is not as easy as it sounds, either.

My husband is not a simple person to make happy. As a dentist in a small town he pretty much sees the same people again and again, which gets kind of old. I at least can listen to the birds sing in the yard or watch television, while he has that drill buzzing in his ears all day. Then again, most people do not like to go to the dentist, and although they try to be nice, dentists can sense this. There is no getting around it that he is an unhappy man. Since this comes mostly from his line of work, I don't think there's much I can do about it, which makes my task of making one person happy each 24 hours that much more difficult. I don't mean to criticize him because we are very comfortable, but that's just my opinion.

For example, when I thought of this happiness idea I couldn't wait for him to get home in order to tell about it. I made a special dinner. Finally the usual time rolled around and he walked through the door. When we sat down at the table I said, "Bob, I figured something out this morning just sitting in the kitchen."

He said, "Well, what?" He got that look on his face that says stop right there. But I went on ahead because I know he gets tired, but I was tired too from making his dinner. He wasn't too tired to eat it, so I figured he owed me that much.

In order to arouse his curiosity I said, "Bob, I know what the meaning of life is."

He took a mouthful and said, "Jean, I don't want to hear this kind of stuff at the dinner table. I have to listen to people all day long, and I don't want to hear this. I wish to Christ you'd go out and get a job, and then you wouldn't have to sit around the whole time just thinking. I know for a fact they need girls out at the fruit-processing plant."

I said, "Bob, it's too bad you don't want to hear me because you might have benefitted."

He said, "Well, I doubt that."

I said, "Well, all right then."

Dear Lord, I don't know how much longer the Earth is going to last, but I do know that if You were to destroy it tomorrow nobody could blame

You. We've messed up Your rivers and streams, and many of us have also messed up our personal lives. When I think back on when I was a little girl it brings tears to my eyes. There was the Mickey Mouse Club and Howdy Doody, and it is hard to believe that I once took those things seriously. Maybe someday I will feel the same way about what I'm doing now. The point is that everything is going off in a thousand different directions. It is frightening to think that someday I will actually be dead. Only You can go on forever, God.

★

Now the guy who delivers our heating oil is a nephew of a fellow that Bob did a lot of work on. In return for Bob going easy on this fellow financially the fellow had a few words with his nephew and the upshot is we get a very good price on our heating oil. Whenever the nephew makes a delivery I always feel like I should invite him in for pie since he plays along with us. This nephew's name is Jack and he's known as Butch.

I don't know if it was the devil's doing, but the next day there was a heating oil delivery.

Butch said, "Well, what's new around here?" He was eating his pie in the kitchen and was in a good mood as usual.

I said, "Butch, what's your philosophy of life?"

He came right back with, "What's yours?" But since I had asked him first he said, "Oh, just to get through the day without doing anybody any harm."

Then I said, "What would you think if I told you the meaning of life was to try to make just one person happy every day.

It doesn't matter if it's an old lady or a newborn baby. Just try to do something for them."

He got real thoughtful for a minute and stopped eating his pie. Finally he said, "Yeah, you might have something there, Jean."

There was something about the way he said it. But I just said, "Yes, I suppose I do."

Then he said, "How about me?"

"What do you mean?" I said.

He said, "You're a good-looking woman, Jean. As far as I'm concerned I'm just out here to deliver the oil. If Bob and Uncle Bill get along real well, hey, that's fine. But I don't owe Bob nothing, it's just an oil delivery to me. But if you want to make some arrangement to make me and you happy, I've never had any complaints."

My mouth just fell open because I didn't know whether to laugh or cry. All I could think of was what if Bob could hear this. He would really blow up. I said, "I didn't mean anything like that at all. You've got a lot of nerve."

He said, "Where did you grow up, Jean? In Muskegon?"

I said, "Yes."

He said, "Well, the women out here don't talk that way unless they've got something on their minds. When they've got something on their minds they start up talking. Don't get me wrong. Maybe I'm way off base and I'm sorry. But you are one good-looking woman, Jean. I'm sorry."

Butch just looked down at his pie. I felt like I was about 12 years old. But the thing of it was, Bob never tells me I'm a good-looking woman. You'd think there was a law against it the way he takes me for granted. I guess Butch could tell what I was thinking because all of a sudden he just grabbed the bull by the horns and said, "I've never had any complaints." He stood up and started rubbing my neck.

We ended up doing it right on Bob's and my bed.

Dear God, I'm not trying to say what I did is right. The road to hell is paved with good intentions, like the saying goes, but that's about all I can tell You. Sometimes when you start out with one thing in your mind you end up with something completely different. I don't mean to hurt Bob and I have got to keep this behind his back, but I have got to get it off my chest too. I am only human. Sometimes I wish we had confession like the Catholics because I would certainly be a regular customer. You are so perfect that it is hard to believe Your creatures are so messed up. All I can say is that I am prepared to suffer the consequences if that is what You want.

⋆

These days when I get in bed with Bob I feel like it is no longer our bed because of what Butch and I have done on it. Plus, if Bob wants something from me in the middle of the night it is all I can do to satisfy him because of what has gone on at that exact spot. Another thing that makes it difficult is that I am so angry at Bob for the way he treats me.

The only way out of this that I can see is for me to get a job. The thing that scares me is that if I'm home alone during the day I start thinking about Butch. After we did it he was a little unfriendly but then he called me up and said, "I thought you said every day." I didn't know what to answer because I wanted to hang up on him in a way and in a way I didn't. Then I thought of the fruit-processing plant. Bob will be happy when he hears I'm going to work at the plant but little does he know.

My advice is to stick with people who think exactly the way you do. You won't get into any trouble. I had a girlfriend like that once and I wonder where she is now. We used to be able to communicate without talking. Another thing is to keep a sense of humor about yourself. Laugh at your problems and they won't seem so big.

Dear God, this is the last thing I have to say. I would like to kill myself but I know that would make You even angrier. I have never begged anybody for anything but now I am begging You. Do You think I should tell Bob what went on between Butch and me? I know You say honesty is the best policy, but half of me feels this is the exception that proves the rule and half of me doesn't. Will You send me a sign of some sort through the weather or a dream? I am crying as I write this although it contradicts what I said about laughing at yourself.

1982

Three Sonnets

1.

I'll drive you to the airport.
Get in the car and I'll
Drive you to the airport.
I'll drive you to the airport.
You want to go someplace?
I'll drive you to the airport.
Come on, let's take a ride,
Pack your bags and
I'll drive you to the airport.
I don't care where you go,
I'll buy the ticket. Seriously,
Because I've had it up to here.
I'll drive you to the airport.
Just don't come back.

2.

Do me a favor. Shut your mouth.
Do us both a favor. Keep your
Mouth shut for twenty minutes.
See if you can accomplish that.
Do me a favor and do yourself
A favor. Twenty minutes is all
I'm asking. Shut your mouth
For twenty minutes. Ten minutes!

Five minutes! Is that too much
To ask? Five minutes of silence.
Is that an impossibility? A fish
On the wall—you never see
A fish on the wall with its mouth
Shut. Which tells you what?

3.

I'm sick and tired of it.
I've had it. I've had enough
Of it. It's gone on too long,
It's taken on a life 'of its own.
It never stops. I literally
Can't take another minute of it.
I'm going to lose my mind if
I have to listen to it again.
Jesus Christ, it never stops
From morning till night,
Day after day year after year.
Do I deserve this? Have I done
Something to bring this on myself?
Oh my God! Dear God help me!

Louis Sisskind, 1891-1962

Leah's shocking death in 1954, then Lou and I
Alone in the labyrinth, four bedrooms,
Four-and-a-half baths, so-called maid's room,
So-called library, so-called butler's pantry,
Fully carpeted, thirty-five-hundred square feet,
Walls like granite, yet cancer had entered
Here as in "The Masque of the Red Death."

Marble nymphs and cupids, brass candlesticks,
Lights in the closets turning on automatically
Whenever the closet doors were opened,
Here a wall-mounted antique brass lantern
From a 19th-century horse-drawn fire engine,
There an amoeba-shaped glass tabletop on
A battleship-gray hunk of shattered driftwood.

Past the unused fireplace and unplayed piano
Each night after eating soup or cottage cheese
Lou and I to the oak-paneled television room
Wended our way, drawn by the electromagnetic
Force of the floor-model Zenith on whose screen
There churned and roiled liquid reds and blues
Of flawed 1950s color television technology.

Passing judgment on Lou, blaming Lou, hating
Him for Leah's painful end-stage renal failure
Of uric acid seeping through her skin, seeing
Him as another blundering President Eisenhower
As we in silence watched *George Burns & Gracie Allen*,
Then *The Lawrence Welk Show,* and at ten o'clock
The Tonight Show Starring Jack Paar would come on.

Yet Lou's own death was not far off. O my father,
How sharper than a serpent's tooth it is to have been
A thankless child. I will watch Jack Paar on YouTube
For three hours, I will dance to Lawrence Welk and the
Champagne Music Makers, I will wear Bermuda shorts,
I will eat a bowl of cottage cheese and sour cream
With crackers crumbled up in it, I will fart, I will snore.

2014

Pursuit of Happiness

The arena: observing combats the Romans fought
Against their own sympathies aroused by scenes
Of mayhem but sympathies quite unbecoming
Citizens of a warfare state. By its cruelty therefore
The howling mob determinedly pledged allegiance
To the authorities' values and symbols or perhaps
They just enjoyed having people tortured to death.
That would be another way of looking at it.

The movies: here also a syrupy rich mix of sadism
And sentimentality offers and often delivers
Have-your-cake-and-eat-it-too experiences of a type
Nowhere else to be found. We observe the lashing
Of a kind and beautiful young black woman at which
The Romans would have laughed but as we watch
The lashing in outrage we feel as good about ourselves
As the ancient Romans felt. Or almost that good.

The Best Western Motel: in 1980 a woman asked
Would I mind if she fell asleep while I made love
To her and I did take offense but now in 2014
The same question from a different woman brings
Nothing untoward and even some little drollery:

‘I’ll be surprised if you don’t.’ Yet she stays awake
And later I do help her to sleep by reciting names
Of college football teams. This is paradise.

2013

I'm Stupid and My Wife is Stupid

I'm stupid and my wife is stupid. Suppose we had a child. The child would be as stupid as the two of us combined. It would be twice as stupid as either of us. What good would the child be to its parents, or to itself? None. On the other hand, we have always wanted to have a child.

Shirley and I talked it over and the conversation went something like this:

"I'd like to have a child that was smart enough to do something besides working like a dog in the plant."

"Smart enough to make a decent living at something."

"It could earn enough money to take care of us when we're old."

"Oh, well, what's the use of kidding ourselves about it, though?"

However, it suddenly dawned on me that I had a friend named Herbert Wilson who was smart. Do you see what I'm getting at?

One night I invited Herbert Wilson over for dinner. After dinner the three of us sat down in the living room to shoot the breeze. Pretty soon Shirley scratched her nose. This was a signal that told me Herbert Wilson was acceptable to Shirley from a physical point of view. She had never met Herbert Wilson before, and she wanted to leave herself a way out in case he happened to be physically repulsive to her. Now, I knew that wouldn't happen because I knew Herbert Wilson was decent looking, kind of tall and thin with a mustache, but Shirley had felt pretty strongly about having some sort of signal. Anyway, the upshot of the whole thing was she scratched her nose.

Then I said, "Herb, you have a reputation around the plant for being kind of a brain. Do you have any idea how high your I.Q. actually is?"

He replied, "Well, when I was in the army they gave us an intelligence test that had seventy-five questions, and I got seventy-three of them right."

Shirley and I looked at each other for a minute as if to say that's good enough for me. Then I said, "Herb, I've got kind of an unusual proposition to make to you. Shirley and I would like to have a child but we'd like it to be halfway intelligent. Since neither of us is exactly a walking encyclopedia, that presents a problem, but we think we've figured a way out of it. Are you at all turned on by Shirley?"

Just like I knew he would, Herbert Wilson said with a little nervous laugh, "Now wait a minute, Larry."

I continued, "Hey, just hear me out, man. If Shirley and I are in the same intelligence bracket, and I impregnate her, that's one thing. But if an individual who is many times as intelligent as I happen to be impregnates her, that's something else again. And nobody need be the wiser."

By now Shirley was giving Herbert Wilson a come-hither look. It was strange to see my wife giving a come-hither look to another male, but this was the price I was going to have to pay. Herbert Wilson shifted around in his chair. I could see we had him a little bamboozled and I said, "Look, as far as anybody will know I'll be the father of the child, and I've been acquainted with you long enough, Herb, to be sure you won't blab this around. Now you may wonder what's in this for you."

"Well, yeah," he answered a little sheepishly but maybe starting to get a kick out of the idea.

Then Shirley said, "Herb, I'm not real smart in the sense of school, but in some other ways I'm a genius." She paraded over and sat on the arm of Herbert Wilson's chair. Next she put one hand on his shoulder. When Herbert Wilson couldn't resist touching her hand she slid right down onto his lap and I knew he was in the bag. I repeat that it was a strange thing to see, but I was mostly pleased about the turn of affairs because I really could not figure another way through our problems.

I stood up and walked over to where they were sitting. I said, "Let's shake hands on this thing being between the three of us and these four walls." He reached around Shirley and we shook.

He said, "Larry, I'm kind of caught off guard by this whole thing. Now I happen to be a guy who's ready to go to bed with a woman any hour of the day or night but, for instance, what if she doesn't get pregnant right off?"

Shirley and I both laughed and I said, "If at first you don't succeed, try, try again, man." Then before he could say another word I continued, "Hey, Shirl and I have talked this out until we're blue in the face. You don't have to do anything or to worry about anything except going into the bedroom and having a good time. Me, I'm going to sit right here and read a magazine. That's how mellow I feel about the whole thing."

I sat down and picked up a *Penthouse* or a *Playboy* magazine, which everybody got a bang out of and which cleared the air.

So they stood up and trotted off toward the bedroom, and by now Herbert Wilson who had admitted to being a horny bastard had part of his hand stuck down the back of Shirley's blue jeans. He looked over his shoulder and took a deep breath and said, "You're an unusual fellow, Larry."

I replied, "Well, maybe so."

Then it was Shirley's turn to look over her shoulder and she silently formed the words "I love you" with her lips, so I silently formed the words "I love you" back.

In a couple of more seconds they were in the bedroom. I heard the door close.

Now it turned out I wasn't quite the man I thought I was because I couldn't just sit there and read the magazine. Pictures of girls, pictures of girls with guys, it was neither the time or the place. I knew any minute I was going to hear the mattress creaking because it's not that far from the living room to the mattress. You may ask why I didn't watch TV. The TV was in the bedroom. If I had been smart I would have moved it into the living room, but if I had been smart none of this would have been necessary in the first place. I finally said to myself, you've got to get out of here, why don't you go outside and take a walk? That's what I did.

Since it was summertime it was still light outside, but things were getting that glow as the sun went down. It was nice and cool too. I walked down the street trying to get my mind off my worries and onto baseball or something, and after a while I came to this park that's a few blocks from our house. There were some kids playing Frisbee with a Labrador dog. I sat down on a bench to watch the goings-on and soon I noticed that someone was walking straight toward me across the grass.

This is where the chain of events becomes hard to believe but bear with me. I will let the chips fall where they may. Here came this person toward me across the grass and it was not long before I realized that it was an incredibly beautiful and sexy young woman in kind of hippie garb consisting of bare feet, faded blue jean cutoffs that were obviously paper-thin from repeated washings leaving nothing about her long tanned legs to the imagination, and a loose-fitting sleeveless blouse embroidered with flowers and birds in many different colors. You could have bowled me over with a feather when she sat down on the bench, smiled, and said, "Hi, Larry, I've got some good news for you. What you and Shirley are doing with Herbert Wilson is the right thing to do, and it's going to work out better than you ever dreamed. The kid is going to be a tremendous genius who's going to think of many new inventions. Not only will these inventions make you a billionaire, but the kid will start a whole era of peace on Earth and good will toward men. Do you know the story of Mary, Joseph, and the angel who talked to Joseph? Well, Shirley's Mary, you're Joseph, and I'm the angel. As for Herbert Wilson, the spirit of the Lord is in him. Ha, ha. You expect emissaries like me to have wings and a white robe, but that was for a different day and age."

I was speechless for a minute but then said, "I don't know the story of Mary, Joseph, and the angel who talked to Joseph."

She replied, "So what? It doesn't make any difference."

I was now speechless again for some length of time and

my mouth must have been open because the emissary seemed amused and said, "You'd better close your mouth before a fly gets in it." Then she sort of got the hysterics for a while from the dumbfounded look on my face. She'd be laughing so hard she was doubled over, and then she'd start to get control of herself, but then she'd laugh again as soon as she looked at me until there were tears rolling down her face. Normally this is the kind of thing that would piss me off if I thought somebody was trying to play a practical joke on me, but I knew that could not possibly be the case here.

Finally she calmed down and asked, "Well, what have you got to say for yourself?"

I said, "I don't think I'm worthy."

She said, "There, there." Then we just sat quietly for a minute.

After a while I asked, "What's supposed to happen now?"

She said, "You've got a little reward coming because this has been a strain on you, some guy in bed with your wife, the Lord's work or no. But let's just say what's good for the goose is good for the gander."

When the emissary saw that I had no idea what she was talking about she moved closer to me on the bench and said, "Larry, you're going to have a sexual experience that you'll remember for a long, long time. I'm going to place a cloak of invisibility over us, we're going to lie down on the grass here, and you'll get an idea of what heaven really is, contrary to common belief." Then she just kind of glided off the bench like a seal or an otter and stretched out on the grass. I'll come back to what happened next later.

By the time I got home it was completely dark out and Herbert Wilson had long since departed. Shirley was in the kitchen drinking a cup of coffee. She said, "Where have you been?"

I said, "Oh, just out for a walk. How did it go?"

"Fine."

"Notice anything unusual about Herbert Wilson?"

She said, "What do you mean by that? Herbert Wilson is a pretty nice person. I think we had better keep this up for several more nights to make sure he impregnates me."

Then I told her what had happened in the park, leaving out my reward however. Shirley poured me a cup of coffee and said with a sigh, "Larry, I think you have been hallucinating. I know you're a very macho person about me, and even though we decided to do this of our own free will it has made you start hallucinating. In a way I'm flattered because it shows you love me, but in another way I'm frightened because I don't want anything to be mentally wrong with my husband. If I end up with a crazy husband, what good is a smart child going to do me? It's impossible for you even to know yet whether I'm pregnant, let alone whether the child will make a billion dollars, and let alone whether Herbert Wilson is God, I'm Mary, and you're Joseph."

I angrily said, "Don't forget that I did not even know the story of Mary, Joseph, and the angel who talked to Joseph!"

She said, "You must have heard it at one time." Then she poured her coffee down the sink and added, "Larry, I'm ready to drop this whole business right now."

I said, "No, no! You ball Herbert Wilson until the cows come home."

She did not interpret this remark the way I intended it and she began to cry. I started to make up to her. Meanwhile, however, I thought about how I knew that what had happened in the park had actually taken place.

Let's go back to when the emissary lay down on the ground. Okay, we started to get it on. Now I've read letters in *Penthouse* or *Playboy* magazine where people say they had this many orgasms, or their girl had that many orgasms, or they did this that and the other thing. Most of those letters are probably not true, but suppose they are. Okay, you take the sexiest one of those letters and multiply it a hundred thousand times and you've got about one one-millionth of an idea of what went on next to the park bench. Ain't nobody can tell me that didn't happen. Plus, I had various grass stains on my pants which proved I must have been down on the grass. Plus, if I was not under a cloak of invisibility but was down on the grass flopping around by myself, then why didn't the kids who were playing Frisbee call the police?

1982

Robert Wisniewski

John and I have worked together a long time. We are the godfathers of each other's children. Every year we get together with a group of guys for a fishing trip and we don't shave for a week.

We are basically the same type of policeman but we like to kid each other. John kids me about how I carry three guns, but we both know it might save John's life someday since he only carries one gun.

We have kicked in some doors together but mostly we just come to work and go home. I would not say we are cynical, but after seeing the underbelly of humanity we don't believe in the Easter Bunny.

We investigated a death on West Wayne Street. A nice two-story townhouse with a parking space in back that was empty so we parked there. We drank coffee in the unmarked car for a while and then went in.

There was smell of smoke on the first floor and balled up wads of burned paper scattered all over. The fire department had been there. Now there were just uniformed police and meat wagon guys.

A body was in the second floor bedroom, a white man about forty named Robert Wisniewski. The consensus of the uniformed police was that he died from inhaling smoke.

Since liquor bottles were lying around in the bedroom we thought maybe he got drunk, passed out, and inhaled smoke from the burned up wads of paper. But who was it that burned those wads of paper?

We found three pages downloaded from an internet dating site, each page with a girl's site profile, her picture, and her name, address, and phone number written by Robert Wisniewski. Great! Fantastic!

We talked to people in the townhouse complex. Did Robert Wisniewski have a family? No. Did he have a car? Yes. What kind of car? One guy said an old muscle car like maybe a Dodge Charger.

The large number of burned paper wads was the odd part. Somebody put time and effort into that and it made a lot of smoke. But burning the house down did not seem to be the idea.

Back in the car we looked at the dating site pages. Three good-looking white girls, Shari, Lexi, and Joy. After we read the profiles and had a few laughs John called Shari and surprisingly she picked up.

John said, "Shari, this is Detective Cronin from the police. Do you know Robert Wisniewski?"

She said, "Um, not really, we just went on one date."

"Well, we'd like to come by and speak with you."

Shari lived in a typical single girl's one bedroom on Surf Street with photos on the refrigerator and shit. She was blonde, medium height, sunny disposition and a decent body as far as I could tell.

We introduced ourselves. Shari offered us coffee. I wasn't sure about her body because she had on a giant sweater that went down to her knees. No shoes, fluffy socks. We declined the coffee.

I said. "Shari, Robert Wisniewski is dead, and it looks like there was some foul play."

"Oh, that's horrible!"

"Well, it happens sometimes," I said with a laugh. "You went out with Robert Wisniewski?"

I showed her the dating site page. "We found this in his apartment, so I gather you met through an online matchmaking site."

She started to cry. "It seems so sordid and sleazy now! I'm so embarrassed!"

Then she got control of herself and said, "We went to Greek Town but it was hard to talk because the restaurant was so noisy. I could tell he liked to drink but I'm not much of a drinker."

I asked Shari if Robert Wisniewski drove her to Greek Town. She said yes he did. "Do you recall what kind of car he had?"

She said, "I'm sorry, I really don't recall."

"That's okay, no problem."

John and I looked at each other. We stood up. I took out my handcuffs. John said, "I'm sorry, Shari, but we have to arrest you for the murder of Robert Wisniewski. Why did you do it?"

The expression on her face was priceless. We laughed and when she saw us laughing she laughed so hard she got out of breath. John gave Shari his business card and we left.

Back in the car I called the next girl, Lexi. She didn't pick up, but we went over there anyway since it wasn't too far and you never know what you're going to find.

Lexi must have had some bucks since her address was an apartment building on North Sherman Road with a doorman, a black kid, behind a desk in the lobby.

Being a black kid, he very quickly picked up that we were

cops, and with that out of the way I mentioned Gene Girolometto of the doorman's union whom I happened to know quite well.

The name Gene Girolometto brought a smile to the black kid's face. The kid must have had something on the ball or else Gene Girolometto wouldn't assign a black kid to Sherman Road.

Was the black kid fucking women in the building? Most likely he was. In any case when we mentioned Lexi it obviously rang a bell. I said, "Do me a favor, call Lexi on the house phone."

When Lexi answered the house phone the black kid said, "There are two gentlemen here to see you from the police department." I motioned for the black kid to give me the phone.

I said, "Hi Lexi, this is Detective Coyne and I'm here with Detective Cronin. We'd like to speak with you about Robert Wisniewski. Remember him? The online dating guy?"

Like Shari, Lexi had only a dim memory of Robert Wisniewski. Unlike Shari, Lexi asked if she could come down instead of us going up because her place was a mess right now.

"No problem," I said and returned the phone to the black kid. John and I then bid him farewell and went to wait for Lexi by the elevator. We just waited. No words were spoken.

This was police work, talking and waiting. You have to like talking and you have to get used to waiting. Now we were waiting and in another minute we would be talking again.

Should we have been a little more inquisitive with Shari, the first girl, because she might be the one who lit the paper wads on fire? No, because Shari had obviously not done that.

Should we have wondered why Lexi, the second girl, wanted to come down instead of us going up? No, because there were a million possible reasons for that and you could go nuts.

Policemen learn not to overly speculate about things but just to move things along and see if things fall into place. Finally the elevator door opened and Lexi came out.

White woman, about five nine, thirties, dark hair, looked grumpy, like if her life depended on it she couldn't crack a smile. Very different from Shari's sunny disposition in that respect.

Running shoes, black stretch pants, sweaty black t-shirt, messy hair, but still a good body from what I could see. Possibly even an excellent body. Her breasts were her best feature.

She launched into a long-winded explanation of how she was in the middle of her treadmill workout and was not prepared for visitors at nine o'clock on a Saturday morning.

The long-winded explanation continued about how she owned a public relations business which was not a nine-to-five job and how precious her workout time was.

John said, "With the demands your job places on you, you probably don't have time to meet guys. That must be why you got on the website and met Robert Wisniewski, right, Lexi?"

"Right," she said. "But I only saw him once."

"Did you go to Greek Town?" I asked. She gave me a look of surprise like, "Are you psychic?" I said, "Just a lucky guess."

"But Mr. Wisniewski is no longer with us," I continued. "His corpse was found in his house when the smoke detectors went off. Would you know anything about that, Lexi?"

She laughed. "Yeah, I hate Greek food, so I fed him a poisoned octopus. Just kidding, boys. If this is what you came to talk about, I can't help you. I know nothing about it."

She wanted to get back to her treadmill. No problem. She kept herself in shape. "But there is still one way you can help," I said. "What kind of car did he have?"

"Car? A Dodge Charger. He was proud of it but it was not my type of vehicle.

I like luxury cars, clothes, and restaurants. When I go to Vegas I stay at the Mandarin Oriental or the Bellagio."

As experienced policemen, we saw that Lexi, like Shari, was in no way responsible for Robert Wisniewski's death. I gave Lexi my business card and we went on our way.

John and I have a system where, if one of us wants to call a woman, he will give that woman his business card and then the other one of us knows to back off.

When John gave Shari, the first girl, his business card I knew to back off and then John knew to back off when I gave my business card to Lexi, the second girl.

In general as luck would have it we have different tastes in women. So when John laid claim to Shari I was cool and he was cool when I laid claim to Lexi by giving her my business card.

Very rarely a situation will arise where both of us are attracted to the same woman. Then some discussion might ensue but that is unusual and we are grownups about it.

It's the same way with driving the unmarked car or making phone calls. One day John drives and the next day I drive. Or if John made the last phone call, then I make the next one.

I was driving when we left Lexi and John called Joy, the last of the dating site girls. She picked up. "Hi Joy, this is Detective Cronin from the police. I've got some bad news."

She said, "Who? What?" John had her on speaker. We were laughing. She sounded a little woozy, like maybe we just woke her up. "Robert Wisniewski is dead!" John shouted.

Then he said, "We're coming right over!" and he cut her off. It was funny. Who knows what she thought. Maybe she would call the police. We were laughing about it.

Joy's place was the top floor of a three-flat. She was around thirty, brunette, a bit on the heavy side, slightly disheveled, clad in blue jeans. Good body. Her ass was her best feature.

Joy let us in and after a brief exchange of pleasantries around the dining room table we made the nature of our visit known. Then there was the usual shock and gnashing of teeth.

There was also the usual dinner in Greek Town story, the disappointment Joy experienced around the whole drinking thing, and her ending the evening early in order to return home.

"Excuse me," I said, "could I use the bathroom?"

"Yes, it's just down the hall."

"Thank you." I did have to pee and after peeing I checked out the medicine cabinet. Nothing special there.

Returning to the dining room I made a side trip into Joy's bedroom and noticed some keys on the dresser. One of the keys had a fancy Dodge Charger logo on it.

Back in the dining room I said, "You're not working today, are you, Joy?"

"No," she said, "I work downtown nine-to-five Monday through Friday like a million other good little sheep."

I nodded sympathetically and said, "Where do you work?"

"I'm the office manager for a group of ophthalmologists called Paul Hurwitz M.D. and Associates Vision Care Center."

At this point John knew something was up or else why would I be acting as if I gave a shit where she worked? I would only do that if I was playing cat and mouse with her.

I said, "When you went to Greek Town with Robert Wisniewski, did he drive?"

"Yes, he did."

"But sometimes people take cabs to Greek Town."

"No, he drove his car."

She gave me a puzzled and nervous look. John was having a hard time keeping a straight face. He knew I was playing cat and mouse but didn't know where the cat and mouse was going.

"Do you remember what kind of car he had?"

"No, I really don't."

"Maybe it was a Dodge Charger."

"Maybe it was."

I took the keys out of my pocket and put them on the dining room table.

"God damn it!" she said. "Fuck! Fuck! Fuck!" She was pounding on the table. She was blubbering. What if she got hysterical?

I sat down at the table. "What happened, Joy?"

"Fuck!"

"Joy . . ."

"Fuck!"

"Joy . . ." She looked at me. Deer in the headlights. "What

happened, Joy?" It was an intimate moment. I started to get hard. But she would have to do about eight years.

"He pissed me off so much!" she said. "A man should realize that when a woman goes back to his apartment with him the woman rightfully expects to get fucked!"

I didn't want her to blow up again. I looked at John. It was his turn. "He wouldn't fuck you?" John said.

"He couldn't fuck me! His prick wouldn't work! He was too drunk!"

Now silence reigned except for her blubbering. We let her cry it out. Finally I said, "When he couldn't fuck you, you went around lighting wads of paper?"

"Yes."

"Why?"

"To make a mess."

That was it. She lit wads of paper to make a mess. It didn't occur to her that Robert Wisniewski, passed out on the bed upstairs, might die from the smoke. That's why it was definitely not a murder charge.

What charge would it be? Some sort of arson maybe. John and I did not need to sort that out. The Dodge Charger was in the forefront of our minds. It was parked down the street from Joy's apartment.

Over the next few weeks several things happened. We determined the book value of the Dodge Charger and we offered to take it off the hands of Robert Wisniewski's next of kin.

On the one hand the next of kin wanted to recoup what the Dodge Charger was worth. On the other hand they saw

Robert Wisniewski as a bum and the Dodge Charger had his cooties.

Ultimately a desire on the part of the next of kin for the whole thing to be over and done with played into our hands. We paid them ten percent below book for the Dodge Charger.

After we had a little work done on the car we were able to sell it for like three times book. We shared the proceeds with our lieutenant and we took everyone else out to dinner.

John wound up fucking Shari and I fucked Lexi a couple of times. A lot of women are turned on by policemen if you're in halfway decent shape, which John and I actually are.

2015

Twenty Questions

There are all sorts of gizmos on the market which defraud the public. Many are sold through the mail. Some, like "Oil Well in Your Sink," are self-explanatory. Another, called "Money Multiplier," looks like a cigarette-rolling machine. Insert a dollar, turn the crank, and a five-dollar bill is promised to appear but doesn't. Many of these contraptions sound funny until you realize that they're making millionaires of con artists, or until you've been bilked yourself. Yes, even I have been bilked.

However, there is one device which really delivers. It's called "Twenty Questions," and looks like an ordinary armchair. In the back of the chair is a small opening. If a photograph or drawing of any person, living or dead, is placed in the opening, that person will appear in the chair to answer twenty questions. And it works. I don't expect you to believe me. I'll prove it to you.

My father died when I was a lad of sixteen. He was seventy-one. During a long night of the soul a few weeks ago I saw that many of my problems could have been avoided if he had lasted a little longer, until I was old enough to understand all that he had to tell me. As the sun rose that morning I noticed an advertisement for "Twenty Questions" in the back of a men's magazine. Not too long afterward the old man sat before me in his paisley bathrobe.

What you are about to read is a complete transcript of my conversation with my father, including information I could not possibly have known myself. Many of my questions—like,

"What was your most important telephone call?"—had been on my mind for years. Others came to me on the spur of the moment. Apart from its emotional meaning to me, the transcript provides a portrait of a man from another time and constitutes a powerful endorsement of the "Twenty Questions" machine, in which I have no equity interest.

1. **You look great. How long have you been dead? More than twenty years . . .**

   Well, as we sit here I've been gone about twenty-two years. I was old when it happened, sick as a dog, sick of being sick, as the advertisement used to say. But that changed fast! I flew out the hospital window as a ghost and soared high above Lake Michigan and the whole city of Chicago. By the time the cleaning ladies, who had been very patient, had finished doing my room in the Kaplan Pavilion, I was swooping like the seagulls you and I used to feed in Florida. You know, swooping reminds me of something. Luminator-Harrison was the first company ever to hold a board of directors meeting on a plane. We used to make the light fixtures for the old Ford Tri-Motor, and during the thirties we held a board of directors meeting on one. It was written up in a magazine. So what, right? And two is eight!

   Anyway, I zoomed and I zoomed. Over on Milwaukee Avenue near the Como Inn, where they used to have strolling violinists, I saw something I'll never forget. The Lloyd Harriss pie factory had caught fire. The flames, the red lights of the fire engines, and the big wet snowflakes were like something from a professional artist's imagination. And for the first time in many, many years I was able just to appreciate that kind of stuff. Even when we used to feed the seagulls, Luminator-Harrison was always in the back of my mind. Only one thing ever really got me away from it while I was alive: the game of pinochle.

2. **And then what happened? I mean, is there some sort of Supreme Being, or merely nothingness?**

Yes, there is a Supreme Being but such a powerful light shines from Him that, even for the dead, looking can be dangerous. As far as His appearance is concerned, all I know is He has the head of a hippopotamus. Let's concentrate on the common, ordinary people. The first excitement of a newly deceased person is allowed to run its course, after which you're guided by specially trained dogs to a sort of depot. There, in the case of a man, your financial records are gone over. See, you get back the body you had during the year of your greatest income. Sounds unfair, but give me a chance to explain. The amount of money earned doesn't matter. Isn't that wonderful? If a guy named Joe made a dime in 1926, and that was the most he ever made, he'll look like he did in 1926. If a guy named Moe won six million dollars at the racetrack when he was eighty-five, he'll be eighty-five again. My best years were right after the war, so I'll always be around sixty years old, and I don't believe in arguing. Now, for women, their appearance is restored to what it was on their wedding day. A lot of people are objecting to that because a girl can be married for one week and divorced the next and still stay young. Listen, there's an old expression: You can't fight City Hall. And women like Birdie Uberflussig, who stayed single, are really frowned upon. They wind up in their late fifties automatically. Go fight City Hall.

3. This may sound strange, but . . .

Don't be afraid. I'm sure we'll get into some very touchy subjects.

What was the most important telephone conversation you ever had?

I can answer that without hesitation. Sometime in the late thirties we got a million-dollar order to manufacture light fixtures for new Pullman cars. Then one morning Elmer Achtboim walked into my office and said, "The guy from the Pullman Company called me at home last night and they're cancelling the order." Elmer, of course, was chairman of the board of Luminator, but the way he figured it he'd already made his money and what he cared about was sailing around the world and art collecting. This is taking nothing away from Elmer. He was, after all, the originator of several new kinds of light fixtures, and he was great at cocktail parties, dinners, or on the golf course. It's just that I had to look at things differently. Well, with Elmer Achtboim standing there, I got on the telephone to Lester Sulloway at the Pullman Company in Pittsburgh, Pennsylvania. He said they were sorry, but they were cancelling the order. After five minutes he said maybe they wouldn't cancel all of it. After about another ten minutes he said they might still have to cancel some of it. Then I hung up the telephone. I said to Elmer, "I want you to catch a plane to Pittsburgh, Pennsylvania. When Lester Sulloway gets to their plant tomorrow morning, I want you to be sitting out front in a car drinking coffee from a paper cup."

Well, to make a long story short, we got the order.

4. What principles did you live by regarding your clothes and your appearance?

All right. The important question for me in deciding what to wear was always, "Am I going to be staying in the house, or am I going out, even if only to take a walk?" If I was going to be in the house I'd wear brown slacks, a short-sleeved sport shirt, and bedroom slippers.

When Bermuda shorts came in starting about 1958, I'd wear them around the house in the summer. I liked to leave them unbuttoned with the fly unzipped because it was more comfortable.

But now let's say that I was going out. That was a whole new ballgame. I rarely went out without a tie, rarely went out without a hat. When I bought a suit it was usually a pretty good one, so I kept all my suits fifteen years. They were always blue or gray. I never owned a brown suit and never owned a brown pair of shoes. When I went out of the house, ninety-five percent of the time it was in a suit.

I was a little unusual regarding underwear. I was devoted to a very light cotton union suit which combined boxer shorts with a sleeveless undershirt in one piece. When these stopped being manufactured, I sent your stepmother Rella running all around the city of Chicago looking for them.

I never wore jewelry, and wore Bulova watches for twenty years at a time. I always had glasses with metal frames, although your mother Pearl tried to get me into more stylish plastic ones when they came in. But my face had a tendency to heat up. It would get so hot that the plastic frames melted out of shape. That's the explanation I gave Pearl, and then I went back to metal frames.

I got a haircut every Friday at Union Station, although I was almost completely bald since 1925.

5. **What was your relationship to the movies and to television?**

I rarely went to the movies, but I always liked television. Right after the war I bought one of the first combined radio-television-phonograph sets in the city of Chicago. I liked to watch baseball and the Groucho Marx quiz show. In my later years, when Lawrence Welk was popular, I enjoyed dancing with Rella while Lawrence Welk played. I liked Jack Paar on account of he wasn't afraid to show his emotions. Which reminds me, if someone cried, as Jack Paar did on several occasions, I would get upset and do anything to make them stop. Once people found out about this, I was probably taken advantage of a couple of times, but so what?

As I said, I didn't go to the movies, but I liked Jayne Mansfield the few times she appeared on TV. Rella and I saw her in person once, too. I didn't like Kim Novak for some reason, but I never saw her except for some photographs in *Time* magazine. I liked Elizabeth Taylor, who looked like a little doll.

6. **You mention Jayne Mansfield, Kim Novak, and Elizabeth Taylor. I'd like to ask about your sexuality.**

My what? What do you mean?

Well, the whole subject of your relations with women, pa.

Hm. I never really had much of a sex life the way many people did, and do. I suppose the main pleasure I got from women, and gave to them, came from making them happy in other ways. And not only women. I liked to make people so happy—usually by buying things for them or by giving them money—so that they'd shut up, or, I should say, be quiet. Let's talk about Pearl for a moment. We got married in 1939. Not long afterward Pearl had part of her stomach removed, but she wanted very badly to have a child. I told her my talents lay elsewhere. However, she wanted a child so much that I said, "Fine. You get somebody, do what needs to be done, and then it will be our child. Let me know when you're pregnant." She got somebody—I still don't know who it was—but then she had a miscarriage. Later she had another miscarriage. After the second one she was so upset in the hospital that I told her, "Don't worry. You're going to walk out the door with a child." I talked it over with Steve Tomato, who had been with Harrison Wholesale a long time and whose wife's family lived out in River Forest. Pearl walked out of the hospital with a child, all right, complete with a birth certificate showing her as your mother. Later, when Pearl died and I married Rella, we got another birth certificate with her name on it.

So you see, I was mainly a businessman. But business can start up a family! Maybe it's just not as much fun. With women, I sometimes liked to snuggle, but mostly I wanted peace and quiet, just like with everything else.

7. **Those are really some surprising facts you've just told me. I mean . . .**

Well, that's what this machine is for. That's its purpose.

I'm going to try to ask about things that are less sensitive. What were your tastes in food?

Again, it depended on whether we're talking in or out of the house. The season of the year was also important. I was a lover of soups, and especially of cold borscht with sour cream during the summer, but only in the house. I rarely ordered soup in a restaurant. On the other hand, I liked frogs' legs, but of course they weren't something you'd eat at home. At the country club I would order frogs' legs.

For thirty years, as long as Luminator-Harrison occupied the building on Washington Boulevard, I ate lunch at the cafeteria across the street. Elmer Achtboim, Peklar Jenknavorian, Hub Snell, and the other big shots liked to go to fancier places, so I usually had lunch alone. When I became diabetic, of course, I had to change my eating habits. I don't know, I can't seem to come up with a real good set of rules about what I liked to eat. Potato pancakes, cottage cheese with sour cream mixed in, shrimp cocktail, Cornish game hen, meat loaf, chop suey . . . there's a time and a place for everything.

8. How about your relationship with automobiles?

Well, that brings up a funny story. I never learned how to drive. I did drive a car a couple of times, but nobody who was there really seemed to enjoy themselves. So Hub Snell, who was a buyer for Harrison, used to pick me up in the morning and we'd drive down to work. Hub was quite an ambitious fellow. He was a good-looking fellow too and his first wife, Tuba, was a beautiful girl who eventually became a prostitute in Miami. Hub's favorite saying was, "Let's get the show on the road." Sometimes when we were driving down to work he would complain that he wasn't moving up fast enough in the company. So I used to say to him, "Look, Hub, you actually run the company. It doesn't matter what your title is. You are the real boss. You carry me around in your arms like a little baby, and not only me. As he sails the Seven Seas, even Elmer Achtboim is somehow being carried around by you."

Then one night I was sitting in the bathtub and Rella came in. I had this wonderful device that I used in the bathtub. It was a sort of mitt that had straw on one side to wash yourself with, and on the other side there were two suction cups. You could attach the mitt to the bathtub and use it as a headrest. That's how I was using it when Rella came in. She said, "Hub Snell is going around the country club telling everybody he runs Harrison Wholesale."

I said, "So what, if it makes him happy?"

She said, "Well, he's got a bigger and newer car than we do." Rella, of course, knew how to drive. I liked to watch her drive and to give her advice.

I said, "Fine. Go get a big new car, and make sure it's four inches longer than Hub Snell's." I always figured that with cars other people knew better than I did.

For instance, when we bought you that used car, which you felt you needed so badly. I thought you didn't know how to drive, but you said you did, so I figured you knew best. Morey Madison paid off the guy at the driver's license place, and eventually you did learn how to drive, by process of trial and error. It's the only way to really learn anything.

9. You haven't said anything about your sisters, although you did mention diabetes before. Didn't your sister Minna have both her legs cut off?

Yes, that's true, of course, that's true. I guess living for so many years with Minna and Myra and their children, after their husbands died, kind of tired me out on them.

They were a little resentful when I married Pearl, and even more so about Rella. Minna's pride and joy in life were her sweet-and-sour meatballs.

Of Minna's two boys, to whom I was, after all, a sort of father, I always felt closer to Benny than to Boris. I think Benny turned out to be more like me. His whole life, for instance, was wrapped up in Harrison Wholesale, and when the company went out of business it was a terrible blow, as it would have been to me. But I died just in time.

Benny was also like me in that he served in the army, while Boris had an asthmatic condition that allowed him to go to the University of Iowa instead. I was never in combat in the First World War, although I did hear the guns going off, but Benny was blown into the top of a tree during the Battle of the Bulge. Then he was in the hospital for quite a while, and now, like the rest of us, he has diabetes. It's a small world.

I often ask myself why Minna and Myra didn't marry again. I think it was because they wanted me to keep taking care of them, which I did, even after I married Pearl. I took care of them financially, and we always had them over for dinner on Friday nights. Minna generally brought a container of sweet-and-sour meatballs, which went straight into our restaurant-size freezer. After dinner, we'd play cards.

10. **How many hours a week would you estimate you spent playing cards, during your peak years?**

The regular Saturday pinochle game, which was an institution for thirty-five years, generally lasted for five or six hours a session. It overlapped for about ten years with a Monday night game four or five hours in length. Friday night card-playing with Minna and Myra, and later also on Saturday nights with Rella's family, was a little different because the game wasn't pinochle. There was a time when I was playing cards about twenty hours per week.

Something went out of our Saturday game, though, when Gustav Goldfish passed on in about 1952. Until then we had been playing at a table set up in Gustav's dry cleaning store. Once we were even raided by the police for gambling. When the game moved to my house, it was more comfortable but less exciting. Don't forget that Moe Kelp drove for two hours to get to the game. For thirty-five years!

My favorite expression while playing pinochle was "For Christ's sake!" which I loved to say with a cigar in my mouth.

11. **What was the *modus operandi* of your cigar smoking?**

I didn't smoke expensive cigars, nor did I smoke many cigars during the course of a day. Both of the cigars

I smoked were Perfecto Garcias: the "Queen," and "Ensign." I was famous for the fact that, when I had finished smoking a cigar, the tip would remain in almost perfect condition. On the other hand, I wouldn't call myself a really neat cigar smoker. I didn't like to use ashtrays, preferring the floor. Sometimes I would make a gesture in the direction of an ashtray, but that would be it. You've got to remember that while I was smoking a cigar I was usually doing something else at the same time—watching Groucho, playing pinochle, or reading the paper.

Generally I smoked one cigar a day, in the evening. On Saturdays I might smoke as many as three.

Neither Pearl nor Rella liked my cigar smoking. Once, when we were down in Florida, Pearl tried to get me to switch to cigarettes, but I didn't like to inhale. Here's the funny part of it: I eventually died of lung cancer.

12. Speaking of pinochle and cigars, do you recall your card tricks, or the way you could make cigars disappear?

Yes, that was a big hit with you kids. I remember going on a Cub Scout hike with you and a whole bunch of kids when I was about sixty-three and doing a lot of cigar tricks. I learned those tricks growing up in the Jewish Orphans' Home, although we used pennies and not cigars. We used to be given one penny a week for good behavior, fifty-two pennies in a year. There was only one day we were allowed outside the walls of the Home, and that was the Fourth of July. If you'd been good, you would have fifty-two cents to spend. That was a lot of money in 1902. I believe most of the men who came out of the Jewish Orphans' Home did very well in the business world.

13. Did your love of sports begin in the Jewish Orphans' Home?

Well, I loved sports mainly as a spectator, not as a participant. But we did play indoor baseball at the Home. In later years I liked to play tennis, to go horseback riding, and to play golf, but I rarely got a chance to do those things. I liked to watch boxing on television.

14. How did you feel about dogs?

You and Rella pulled a fast one on me, getting Matzoh while I was in the hospital for my prostate operation. In my weakened condition I wasn't able to object too much. I did come to love Matzoh. She used to jump on my stomach, and, of course, she did outlive me.

We had never had animals in the Home, and I didn't really know how to act around them. Also, I didn't really want to compete with a dog, a cat, or a bird for anyone's attention.

It was after my prostate operation that I really started to slow down. I was sixty-six years old, and I'd been working non-stop, supporting people, since I got out of the Home more than fifty years earlier. I started taking naps after work and sometimes coming home early.

15. This coincided with the gradual decline of Luminator-Harrison, didn't it?

That's true. In 1958, Luminator failed to get the order for the fixtures on the Boeing 707. I went out to Seattle myself, but we lost the order. Harrison Wholesale was being hurt by the rise of the discount stores. They were located in shopping centers, while the idea of Harrison Wholesale had been to make people look for it, make them think they'd really discovered something. Elmer Achtboim had already stepped aside. He'd turned over his role in the company to his son, Horace, who weighed almost four hundred pounds, and to his son-in-law, Burt Clovis, a graduate of the Harvard Business School. It was at Burt Clovis's suggestion that we purchased the largest warehouse in the city of Chicago, which we couldn't possibly have used. Burt was one of the first businessmen in Chicago to wear the new flattop haircut, by the way.

16. How was Horace Achtboim's weight a liability to the company?

As I said earlier, the wonderful thing about Elmer was his behavior at dinner parties, cocktail parties, and on the golf course. Horace didn't like to drink because it was fattening, but he ate too much at dinner parties for the same reason. He couldn't play golf. We really needed somebody with all the social graces. I was never good at that and was too old anyway. As for Burt Clovis, everybody could see right away that he was a phony.

17. You speak of these things with such vehemence! That, and the way your health and the company's declined at the same time, sometimes give me the feeling that business was all that really mattered to you. But there's so much more to life, like . . .

I agree with you, I agree with you one hundred percent. But as I said at the beginning, it was only after I died that I really allowed myself to enjoy many of these things. I must say, also, that many people were able to enjoy them because I was too busy.

When Tuba Snell was breaking up with Hub, she came over to the apartment. It was on a Sunday. We went into a room and closed the door. She said, "I want to leave Hub and move to Miami with a fellow I met. What do you think I should do?"

I said, "If that's what you want, then you should do it."

She said, "The fellow doesn't have any money. Will you pay for everything, lock, stock, and barrel?" So I did.

It wasn't my idea, but there were times when I enjoyed the fact that, when I gave some money to the hospital to build a laboratory, it turned out to be a laboratory for tapeworm research.

18. I must say, since we're getting near the end here, that I'm starting to resent the way you keep patting yourself on the back.

Is that a question?

All right. Let me see if I can trap you. What was the biggest mistake you ever made?

I really don't know. Again, thinking about mistakes was a luxury I never allowed myself. I just tried to think about the good and not concentrate on the bad. That's why I never read books, which often deal with problems. Aren't you going to ask me for some advice?

19. Will you give me some advice?

Yes. Be very careful about trusting a short man, because the other half of him is often operating under the ground, so to speak. Also, short men often wear bow ties, and be very careful of a man who wears one.

You seem to be becoming a bit angry.

Maybe a little tired. It's something that never changes.

20. We're at the end anyway. Is there anything you'd like to leave me with?

Well, I mentioned before about watching boxing on television. I'll never forget one night Manny Organic was at the apartment, and we were watching a boxing match. Manny was famous for two things. Whenever he met a new person, he let them know right away that he was a lawyer. He'd say, "Hello, I'm Manny Organic, I'm a lawyer." He also liked to ask married couples how they met. He felt it was a good way to get to know people. A lot of times he'd get some nice conversations going.

Anyway, one night we were watching a boxing match, and it was the last round, and these two guys were really letting each other have it. Then the bell rang. They put their arms around each other and started hugging. Manny actually threw my cigar across the living room. He said, "That's the most beautiful thing. Fight, but don't get mad." And yet it was said of him that if he told you the time, you'd get a bill in the morning.

Thank you.

You're welcome.

1982

The Apparition

No two people are alike, and no two horses are alike, but certain people are very much like certain horses. Dennis Panitch thought about it as he put on his rented tuxedo. In Dennis's neighborhood, the men followed horse racing. They won a little money or lost a little. As a boy Dennis had begun going to Sportsman's Park with his father, and now he went there on his days off from the furniture-moving truck.

Born to Be Wild blared from a cassette player as Dennis remarked, "Ray, now I'm betting everything on one horse, man." He felt slightly giddy in the brash, locker-room atmosphere they had created. Ray Burns was going to be best man. He was in the room to help Dennis with the cummerbund.

Ray said, "Don't let Lisa hear you talking about her like no horse," but then he laughed, "Jovial Poker!" It was the name of a local racehorse.

Dennis laughed, "Water Rhumba!"

"Jovial Poker!"

After the ceremony there was a party at Sub and Eileen's house. Eileen was Lisa's sister. Sub, her husband, worked for the city and had promised to help Dennis get a job. As people crowded into the living room, Sub moved some lamps onto the stairs, to create more space and to prevent anyone from going to the second floor, where a baby was asleep. Another child ran among the guests pulling a toy lawnmower. Loud talk reverberated off the ceiling. Dennis's mother—his father had been dead for several years—chatted happily with Lisa's parents. Lisa herself stood beside the groom holding his hand and occasionally leaning her head against his shoulder. She had gotten her hair cut into what she called a gypsy shag.

Sub had paid for a room that night in a new hotel near the airport. Dennis would have liked a real honeymoon, but it would have to wait until, say, he passed the fire department examination. He stood before the mirror and removed his ruffled shirt. He had a good build, he felt young and strong. During one section of the fire department examination the candidate must drag around a two-hundred-pound sandbag, but Dennis actually looked forward to that. He hung the tuxedo in a closet. He climbed into bed and waited for Lisa to come out of the bathroom. Now it was quiet except when a plane passed over. Where was the cassette player now?

Oh, where were the girls various rock-and-roll songs reminded him of?

Lisa came out of the bathroom. She was wearing a nightgown of fine white lace. It lay lightly on her body, like ice forming over water. She had bought it the afternoon her hair was cut.

Sitting on the bed beside Dennis, she touched his hand. There was a long, quiet moment. It continued. Finally Lisa said, referring to the nightgown, "This is supposed to turn you on."

"Just give me some slack. I'm turned on," Dennis told her, as a plane roared overhead.

When it was gone, Lisa declared, "You could have fooled me, man." Dennis said nothing. Another silent time began. When the price of the nightgown occurred to Lisa, she stood up, began to cry, and ripped the gown from the neckline to the hem. Here was a fiery girl, one still remembered at the high school she had attended. She shouted, "I'll give you some slack! Here's slack!"

"Hey, baby." Dennis got up from the bed.

"Here's . . ."

"Hey . . ."

How he missed his father sometimes. Once they had taken the train to Arlington Park, to see the great Buckpasser run. His father had bet everything on that horse, all he had and whatever he could borrow. They watched Buckpasser come from last, from twenty lengths off the pace, to set a record in the mile. Baeza was the rider. In Dennis's mind the names of champions shone among those of the other horses like constellations in a black sky: Nashua, Citation, Damascus, Never Bend.

He put his arms around Lisa. Her wet face pressed against his chest. Looking over her shoulder, Dennis thought he saw the ghost of his father across the room. He lowered his eyes, bent to kiss his wife on the ear, but when he looked up the ghost was still there. Its smile seemed to tell him that everything would be all right when he got a better job.

1979

Leo Manasin

Drilled through the *kishkes* in '44
He subsequently worked for
The old Central Electric Company
On Washington Boulevard until
Mr. Achtboim died in 1956.
Then came what Leo and Ruth Manasin
Always called the cow magnet years.

Cow magnets: bits of iron swallowed
By cows to which adhered any
Gum wrappers, bailing wire, nails,
Or what have you that a grazing cow
Might ingest, thereby creating a mass
Of sufficient bulk to travel through
The digestive system of the cow.

It was the brain child of Jim Porter,
A Wisconsin veterinarian who said,
'I got tired of tramping barnyards
On cold mornings to vaccinate hogs
At five dollars a shot, so I dreamed up
The cow magnet. They said I was crazy
But with a hundred million cows

'In America the dairy and beef industries
Would pay two bucks per magnet to keep
A herd of cows from coming down
With the so-called Hardware Disease.'
Not long after Mr. Achtboim passed away,
Steve Drago introduced Jim Porter
To Leo Manasin at Nippersink Manor.

At that time a sort of black cloud seemed
To hover over Leo Manasin's head.
Although Mr. Achtboim was no saint,
He was the *pater familias* that Leo Manasin
Needed in the post-war years when lingering
Effects of his wounds imbued every moment
With a vague unconscious sense of dread.

Now this man Jim Porter entered the picture.
Here was a new pater familias, possibly
An improved version of Mr. Achtboim,
Who offered Leo Manasin the position
Of cow magnet sales rep for the Wisconsin,
Illinois, and Indiana territories in which
Resided tens of thousands of cows.

But Leo Manasin hesitated. He ruminated.
He looked skeptically at a future in which
He would call on dairy farmers with

A satchel of cow magnets in his lap while
Over a blue propane flame water boiled
For instant coffee in farmhouse kitchens
Of stained linoleum and peeling wallpaper.

He was a city boy after all, a Jewish fella
Whose occasional exposure to anti-Semitism
Made him leery of many (not all) *goyim.*
Jim Porter seemed like an honest *goy,*
And now Jim Porter allayed Leo Manasin's
Fears about the future with some simple
Truths about the cow magnet business.

As the veterinarian explained, most magnets
Were bought in bulk by feed company
Executives over lunch in the grill room of
The Cliff Dwellers Club where past members
Included Cyrus McCormick, George Armour,
And Rufus C. Dawes, and not bought by farmers
With a load of manure out in the dump truck.

This mollified Leo Manasin and he was soon
Turning heads in the cow magnet industry.
Sales of a hundred or two hundred gross
Were run of the mill for Leo Manasin
In the grill room of the Cliff Dwellers Club
And it was there that he met Chester Schultz,
The heir to a milking machine fortune.

Chester Shultz shrewdly took the measure
Of this family man named Leo Manasin,
This war veteran who sold cow magnets
For a living and—liking what he saw—
Chester Schultz took Leo Manasin under
His wing and began making discreet
Overtures to Leo Manasin about a job.

These discreet overtures, these coy hints,
The innuendoes, the asides, the ingratiating
Small confidences, the verbal nosegays,
The *divertimenti*—they also had a deeper
Purpose, a much more sober intention.
The discreet overtures were the foundation
For the hiring of Leo Manasin by Chester Schultz.

It was a very nice employment package that
Chester Schultz offered with substantially
Larger revenues to Leo Manasin in exchange
For less work—because once milking machines
Were leased out there was nothing to do
Except deposit the checks which would represent
Leo Manasin's salary plus a generous commission.

And since milking machine leases were always
Rolled over, Leo Manasin could be set for life!
A home in Lincolnwood on a double lot,
A Buick, an Olds, or even a Cadillac convertible

In the garage; a country club membership;
And a summer house in Sauganash, Michigan;
All this was possible with Chester Schultz!

Only one small matter remained: Jim Porter
Must be told of Leo Manasin's decision to forsake
His *pater familias* and cleave to this wealthier
Man named Chester Schultz, this man whom
Leo Manasin met at the very Cliff Dwellers Club
Where Jim Porter was footing the bill for
Leo Mansain's lunches of broiled whitefish.

But then occurred one of the eerie
Turning points that we encounter in life,
One of the head-scratching moments
In which our decisions seem to be made
By some external agency and we can only
Look back on the decisions as they fade
In the rearview mirror of our years

Like a roadside restaurant where we ate
Something but what exactly did we eat?
This eerie turning point in Leo Manasin's life
Occurred at the *bar mitzvah* of his son Mickey
At Temple B'nai Zion on Pratt Avenue
Where Leo Manasin had *naches*—that is, pride
In his child—as he made small talk with Jim Porter.

This was in the hospitality room where,
After the ceremony, cold cuts were being served.
There Leo Manasin felt an unexpected surge
Of emotion, a cresting wave of affection
For the man named Jim Porter, and all at once
It seemed unimaginable to Leo Manasin that
He could ever disassociate himself from Jim Porter.

What caused the unexpected surge of emotion?
First, it was Jim Porter attending the *bar mitzvah*
And also the sight of Jim Porter wearing a *kippah*,
A *yarmulke*. In fact, the sight of Jim Porter wearing
A *kippah* was a great honor to the Manasin family
As a whole: to Leo, Ruth, Mickey, and Melissa,
Who was also known as Missy or Lissie.

The remarkable thing was how comfortable,
How relaxed Jim Porter looked, as if he'd
Worn a *kippah* all his life. Whereupon
It occurred to Leo Manasin that perhaps
The veterinarian could convert to Judaism.
There could be *bar mitzvah* for Jim Porter
And if necessary he could be circumcised.

What a mitzvah it would be for Leo Manasin
To bring about the conversion of Jim Porter
To Judaism! The thought of Jim Porter reciting

The *sh'ma* almost brought tears to the eyes
Of Leo Manasin—and Jim Porter also seemed
Sensitive to the moment. He spoke not a word
But put his hand on Leo Manasin's shoulder

And guided Leo Manasin toward a quiet
Corner of the B'nai Zion hospitality room.
There in a voice charged with feeling,
Jim Porter said to Leo Manasin, 'Leo,
I want you to know that come what may
In the cow magnet business, regardless of
What happens in the cow magnet business,

No matter what may or may not occur
In the cow magnet business, good or bad,
You and your family will be taken care of
Forever because of the hard work and
Loyalty you've given to the organization
Since that day at Nippersink Manor when
We were introduced by Steve Drago.'

Late that night, after the gala celebration
In the Hyatt at 4500 West Touhy Avenue,
After all the singing and all the dancing
And the many clever toasts, Leo Manasin
Lay awake as a voluptuous sense of relief
Washed over him, subsuming even his
Naches about Mickey Manasin's *bar mitzvah*.

The phrase 'dodged a bullet' occurred
To this man who'd been drilled through
The *kishkes* in '44. He saw that a personal
And professional catastrophe had nearly
Happened when he came so close
To deserting Jim Porter, that *mensch*,
By going to work for Chester Schultz.

What a mess that would have made.
What a train wreck it would have been.
It would have been like a twelve-car pileup
On the interstate during the rush hour.
It shouldn't happen to a dog, and fortunately
It didn't happen. Willy-nilly, Leo Manasin
Had made the right decision in the end.

So the cow magnet years continued and
To his credit Chester Schultz took no
Offense at what for him was the very
Unaccustomed experience of a rejected
Job offer. Leo Manasin and Chester Schultz
Even took steam together occasionally
In the Cliff Dwellers Club steam room.

And Jim Porter's conversion to Judaism?
Leo Manasin now saw it as a harebrained
Scheme, heartfelt and well-intentioned,
But brought on by the emotional turmoil

In which Leo Manasin found himself that day
Amid the *bar mitzvah's* hugger-mugger and
The hurly-burly of the Chester Schultz affair.

No, Leo Manasin was not leading the most
Exciting life but as long as there were
Cows there would be cow magnets
And for that he had Jim Porter to thank.
'Leo, come what may,' Jim Porter had said,
'You will be taken care of—you and Ruth
And Mickey and little Melissa Manasin.'

But 'always' is such a long time
About which to make promises—
And must not 'always' always end?
One day Leo Manasin arrived
At the modest downtown office
Maintained by Jim Porter and
Found two men waiting at the door.

Since Leo Manasin had come downtown
To meet a couple of buyers from the
William M. Glass Company, he asked,
'Are you the guys from William M. Glass?'
They said, 'No, we are the guys from
The Internal Revenue Service but
You may call it the IRS if you prefer.'

Thus concluded the cow magnet years
And thus did 'always' come to an end.
It was not for lack of effort on
Jim Porter's part but understanding
The digestive system of a cow is not like
Running a business where the damn
Complexities can make your head spin.

It did not happen all at once. For weeks,
Months, almost a year the cow magnet
Business stayed more or less afloat but
What with judgments and liens and even
The possibility of a criminal case against
Jim Porter brewing, Leo Manasin saw
That the party was over once and for all.

Nights Leo Manasin lay awake kicking
Himself, asking himself why, why, why?
The image of Chester Shultz appeared
Like a ghost in the darkness, mocking him,
Making faces at him and tossing money
Into the air or feeding it to some obnoxious
Animal—a cow?—that he'd brought along.

Mornings Leo Manasin was agitated,
Irritable, he couldn't sit still to read
The newspaper, yet at the same time

He was exhausted and often fell asleep
In front of the television set. He snapped
At people for no reason but also wept
Uncontrollably in the laundry room

Where, pathetically, the washing machine
Drowned out his sobs. This was a far blacker
Cloud than the cloud that hovered over
Leo Manasin's head when Mr. Achtboim died.
This cloud rapidly descended and engulfed
Leo Manasin until he became invisible
To his own family in his own home.

Meanwhile Mickey Manasin became obsessed
With motorcycles, literalizing his desire
To escape the Manasin family's dismal
Twenty-eight-hundred-square-foot home
In favor of the open horizons celebrated
In the Bob Seger anthem 'Against the Wind'
Which he kept blaring in the garage all day.

Melissa Manasin was now called Mel.
Missy? Lissie? Are you kidding me?
At seventeen Mel radiated a hard,
Wised-up sexuality that scared away
The high school boys, so she blew off school
And worked downtown at the Furniture Mart
Where at least a few guys knew how to fuck.

As for Ruth Manasin, she mourned her life's
Reduced circumstances, a life now sustained by
Social security and the savings accounts which,
Thank God, she had insisted on opening during
The cow magnet years. As Ruth mourned,
She saw too how Leo Manasin was suffering,
Was deteriorating, was no longer the same man.

Money alone could not account for his misery,
Ruth Manasin concluded. The black cloud that
Now engulfed Leo Manasin seemed like it had
Always been there and always would be there.
Cow magnets, aging, even disappointment
In the children could not begin to explain what
Ruth Manasin observed each day in Leo Manasin.

He lay on the sofa, defeated and deflated,
In boxer shorts and undershirt. By the way,
He'd lost a leg to diabetes. His snoring briefly
Seemed louder as Ruth Manasin turned off
The television set, but then came a diminuendo
In the snoring until there was only the low
Rumble of the refrigerator motor in the kitchen.

Perhaps we haven't really gotten to know
Ruth—but a favorite expression of hers was
'I have news for you' and another was
'Let's call a spade a spade.' In that spirit

(Though it broke her heart) she now saw
Leo Manasin as a lovable *schmuck*,
A *putz*, a wounded veteran whose wounds

Never really had a chance to heal before he went
To work for the old Central Electric Company
And found a *pater familias* in Elmer Achtboim
And then another *pater familias* in Jim Porter.
But essentially he was a tearful little boy
Desperately looking for someone to protect him
Which caused him to make a really terrible

Business decision about Chester Schultz.
Though he had been a good provider in the
Cow magnet years, she felt that Leo Manasin
Had let his heart get in the way of his head
About Jim Porter. Then it went all belly up.
She loved Leo Manasin but she mainly felt sorry
For him like on *All My Children* or *One Life to Live*.

As Leo Manasin opened his eyes Ruth loomed
Above him, upside down from his viewpoint
But an angelic vision of a benevolent old woman.
Could this be his grandmother, whom he had
Called the *Buba*? Then came a cresting wave
Of emotion like that other cresting wave
At the *bar mitzvah* when Jim Porter had said,

'Leo, you will always be taken care of.'
How loved he had felt then and also now,
With the TV off, the thankless children gone.
As is our destiny at the moment of death
He was changed into a great *tzaddik*
Who reveals himself at last, and at last
Is to himself revealed. *'Sh'ma Yis'ra'eil . . .'*

With his final breath he proclaimed the *sh'ma*!
No mitzvah is greater than this one! Thus did
Rav Shimon bar Yochai depart this life
And thus did Leo Manasin also depart it!
'Sh'ma Yis'ra'eil Adonai Eloheinu Adonai Echad!'
His soul swept past the Heavenly Tribunal
And was received at once into the Upper Worlds!

2011

Grrrrr!

There are two kinds of intelligence, the kind you get out of books and the kind you are born with or not, which I call common sense, horse sense, or being street smart. The second kind is more valuable, and I have it, which is why I have been successful.

Some people will say, "But you are not successful. You don't have a fancy car, you don't have a big house, and you don't have a lot of money in the bank."

I will tell those people, "I am a Zen Buddhist and a karate expert, which means I only want the practicalities. Also, I have the best thing there is, which is a good-looking wife."

A good-looking wife! What more do you want? I got her using street smartness, not knowledge you get out of books or with large numbers of material things. I will prove that this is what turns women on (street smartness, being macho, etc.).

Darlene was going with a guy named Bill Smith when I met her, which was at a cocktail party someplace where I stood out like a sore thumb because I didn't know anybody. I was standing in the corner pulling on a beer when this beautiful blonde came in with Bill Smith, who was wearing an expensive suit, expensive loafers, and a gold watch. But this voice inside me said, "You can make mincemeat out of him." So I decided to ask Darlene to dance.

That's the way I am. If I see something I want, I take it. Why am I on this earth? For my pleasure, not anybody else's.

So I walked up to Darlene and asked her to dance. Bill Smith was standing there but he was helpless. Darlene looked at him as if to say, "Well, what the hell?" but I knew she was only putting on an act and that she really wanted to dance with me pretty bad. I am thirty-nine years old, five-ten, about one-eighty-five, with glasses. She was about twenty-two years old, with blonde hair (as I said before) down to the middle of her back, and with a great body plus a great face.

After we had danced and had found out each other's names she said, "Roy, I better get back to Bill Smith, I guess."

However, I told her, "Who is this Bill Smith? Oh, I get it. You are hanging out with him because of his money. There are some things you can't buy with money."

"Like what?"

I went on, "Let's say I had a private helicopter. Fine. Now what am I going to do with my private helicopter when I'm not using it? Or what if I get tired of flying around in it? It'll get to be a pain in the ass. So what do I need with a private helicopter, or three Ferraris, or a mansion? I travel light."

Darlene said, "I see what you mean. I like you because you are macho without being too macho."

We kissed and then got out of there. We went to my apartment and after a non-stop all-night lovemaking session she told me again she liked me. She said, "You both physically and mentally turn me on. I want to live with you here."

Only at that time I was not ready to be tied down, which I told her, and we bid each other a tearful-on-her-part goodbye.

End of Part One of the relationship.

Part Two of the relationship began at another ritzy cocktail party where I did not know anybody. Darlene came in with this guy named George Peterson who was bald and who tried to act like an Einstein. Darlene and I recognized each other and quickly came toward each other in the center of the crowded room as if we were magnetized. We again danced and kissed.

Then I said, "Who is this guy George Peterson? Oh, don't tell me on account of I already know: Mr. Brain. When a guy like that takes an I.Q. test he does fine, but if you put him out on the street and asked him to survive he couldn't do it. That type of person is so smart they outsmart themselves in real life. But I could survive because there are lots of guys who know me on the street, and even if I was somewhere where nobody knew me I could still survive, with karate."

I didn't even have to say, "Let's get out of here," because Darlene said it herself. We went to my apartment and had another non-stop all-night lovemaking session. In the morning I realized I was now ready to be tied down, so I proposed and Darlene said, "Yes."

Some people will say, "This is all bullshit. You probably don't know karate or anything about Zen Buddhism, aren't macho at all, and are a virgin sitting in a room someplace having your fantasies. You probably don't have any money, so you invent stories about beautiful girls falling in love with you. The whole thing doesn't sound believable. You said yourself that you are five-ten and one-eighty-five, which is probably all fat, so why would a beautiful girl want to go to bed with you immediately? Plus, what did you do that was so street smart, except talk, which can be done by anybody?"

I will tell those people, "I don't want to come down to your level, so I won't argue with you, but I have a little surprise for you. I can see Darlene right from where I am sitting. She is wearing a blue bathrobe with nothing on underneath. I am going to let *her* prove what I have said. I am going to let *her* tell anybody who doesn't believe me that they can go to hell. She is begging and pleading for me to let her do this."

This is Darlene. I have had bit parts in two movies and have starred in commercials. I could have any man I want but I want Roy, partly for the reasons he has stated, which are true, but mainly for something else. It is mainly that he really loves me. One time after we had sex he said, "If you threw up, I would eat it," which was gross but I knew what he was trying to get across. Another time he said, "I always want to be with you. Even when we die I want to be buried in the same grave with you." When you accuse him of being a liar and a bullshitter it gets me so mad that I want to scratch your eyes out. Grrrrr! Because even if I were a figment of a person's imagination, which I'm not, I think just making me up deserves a lot of credit. But on second thought I want you to go ahead and call me a figment! I will have the last laugh because I think the same thing about you. Then I will laugh and you will cry. I am laughing now.

1982

Like a Monkey

Our sages tell us Rachel was a beautiful woman.
Light brown hair brown eyes
Five feet six or seven
Not a clothes horse
But always looked great whether getting ready for work
In white cashmere sweater pleated navy skirt
Or in the bleachers at a Cubs game
In cutoffs and t-shirt
Yet beside Sarah our sages tell us
Rachel was like a monkey
Rachel was like a monkey beside Sarah.
For our sages tell us Sarah was a beautiful woman
And most of all she loved to dance.
People try to move too much she said
Diamonds and rust on the stereo
Really you don't even need to move your feet.
You don't even need to move at all
Or just a little really
Yet beside Eve our sages tell us Sarah was like a monkey.
Sarah was like a monkey beside Eve.
For our sages tell us Eve was a beautiful woman
She dyed her hair to a metallic purple sheen
Wore matching purple eye shadow
And silver jewelry
Goth look but she made it work,

Teardrop tattoo by left eye
So small you might not even notice
And to the surprise of many she majored in cosmology
Physics journals on the floor
In her bathroom by the toilet
Yet beside Adam our sages tell us Eve was like a monkey
Eve was like a monkey beside Adam.
Beside Adam's foot our sages tell us
Eve was like a monkey
His foot shining brighter than the sun
Brighter than a thousand suns
Flash across the just-created sky
Fission burn
Of which though hidden,
A single spark still burns in you.

2009

Joe Adamczyk

He was Joe Adamczyk and
Eve Grabuskawa was her name.
They owned a tavern called
Adamczyk & Eve's and they
Called their sex life Grandma Fogarty.

Nights as closing time approached
Joe would say, 'Eve, do you think
Grandma Fogarty could drop by?'
And Eve would often answer,
'I would not be a bit surprised.'

Years passed in just this way.
Blatz, Schlitz, Pabst Blue Ribbon,
Heileman's Old Style Lager,
Old Milwaukee—ten thousand
Beer glasses filled and emptied.

When pizza pies, as they were then known,
Achieved popularity Joe and Eve offered
The pies to customers and called them
Polish pizzas for a laugh. Beer sales
Skyrocketed as pizza pies appeared.

Also available were White Owl cigars,
And Cubs' home runs were called
White Owl Wallops by Jack Brickhouse
On the TV set above the bar.
But the Cubs lost during the 1950s.

In those days some wrong ideas were held.
Around the time Kennedy was elected and
When Eve Grabuskawa began her menopause,
Grandma Fogarty was told to take her leave.
Grandma Fogarty was sent on her way.

No more did Grandma Fogarty come calling
At all hours of the night like a will-o'-the-wisp
Fluttering, flickering, and then fully ablaze.
As Eve and Joe's union passed twenty years,
Grandma Fogarty was nowhere to be found.

But is this not a familiar story as married
Couples age and passion's flame sinks?
Let us turn to the much more novel story
Of how Joe Adamczyk, the Chicago bartender,
Transformed himself into a man of ideas.

No stale autodidact would he become,
But a thinker comfortable and at home

In a variety of disciplines, reading widely
In libraries, copying pages, memorizing
Long passages, and making diagrams.

He would hardly sleep. He ate little and,
As was true of Edmund Burke,
Anyone trapped under a tree with him
In a sudden rain would quickly see
That Joe Adamczyk had a first-rate mind.

With time his interests would encompass
Gottlob Frege and Whitehead and also
Alonzo Church and Church's dissertation,
Awarded at Princeton in 1927, entitled
Alternatives to Zermelo's Assumption.

His transformation began inauspiciously,
Meandering for years like a stream.
Paint-by-numbers was his first awakening:
Sunsets, views of old windmills,
Solitary reapers, the heads of noble steeds.

In faux-impressionist style these emerged
From the confusing higgledy-piggledy
Of lines and numbers on canvas glued
To cardboard. Joe could execute a large
Paint-by-numbers landscape in one day.

Somehow from his paintings a hunger
For narrative gradually developed.
He imagined stories of people who
Lived in his paint-by-numbers cabins
With smoke curling from the chimneys.

Fascinated by the concept of man
As a storytelling animal, he began
Serious reading for the first time in his life.
He read *The Caine Mutiny* by Herman Wouk
And *Marjorie Morningstar*, also by Wouk.

He followed Wouk with the historical novels
Of Irving Stone: *Lust for Life, Men to Match*
My Mountains, and *The Agony and the Ecstasy.*
He read the best-selling *Magnificent Obsession*
And *The Big Fisherman*, both by Lloyd C. Douglas.

He amused himself by considering life
As a stage play. Tragedy or farce?
He pondered the nature of storytelling,
Then took the short leap, intellectually,
To viewing the world itself as a narrative.

Turning his attention to non-fiction,
In Volume Two of Will and Ariel Durant's
The Story of Civilization he discovered

The concept of *telos* in a discussion of
Greek philosophy and Aristotle.

He gnawed at the concept of *telos* like a dog
With a bone. He toyed with the caprice
That even mathematics might be teleological:
An unwinding tale with a start, a middle,
And perhaps an end returning to the beginning.

He grew careless of his tavern and
Heedless of Eve Grabuskawa, still his wife.
He felt drawn to the used bookstores
And hole-in-the-wall coffee houses
Near the University of Chicago.

The day came when without a word
Joe left Eve Grabuskawa and rented
A room on South Harper Avenue.
He immersed himself in the collegiate
Ambience of the University.

In a coffee house called the Pegasus
He saw a reproduction displayed
With ironic intent of the portrait
Entitled *Arrangement in Grey and Black*,
Also known as *Whistler's Mother.*

He was shocked, set back on his heels
By the subject's strong resemblance
To Eve Grabuskawa. Had all those years
Of marriage to Eve Grabuskawa been
A dour arrangement in grey and black?

It was the last time he ever thought
Of Eve Grabuskawa, who evanesced
Like the Cheshire Cat and even his
Attraction to women in general
Deliquesced like Frosty the Snowman.

Yet the Pegasus was known for pulchritude.
It was the era of girls in black turtlenecks
With love for jazz and folk music—
Educated young women who watched
Italian films at the all-night Clark Theater.

There in the Pegasus one of those women
Approached Joe, she stole up behind him,
And in a voice rich with a kind of sarcastic
Academese she asked, 'Have you read
The Dialogues of Alfred North Whitehead?'

Joe's look of baffled incomprehension
Must have moved or amused her,

For she pressed a dog-eared paperback
Into his hand: the 1956 Mentor Classics
Edition of Whitehead's *Dialogues.*

'Here, take my extra copy,' she said,
Slinking out of the Pegasus as Joe
Glanced at the book's cover illustration
Of Whitehead reading aloud from a
Volume held in his liver-spotted hands.

What a revelation *The Dialogues of*
Alfred North Whitehead proved to be!
That very night, like a magic carpet,
The book whisked Joe from his bare room
To Whitehead's home in Cambridge.

There, close by Harvard Yard, a journalist
Named Lucien Price drew the eminent
Mathematician into conversation ranging
Across history, theology, philosophy,
Politics, education, and of course mathematics.

A truly fascinating man was Whitehead,
In Joe's opinion, a man full of surprises.
He believed, for example, that mathematics
Beyond quadratic equations should remain
The province of specialists—and Joe agreed.

As a teenager Joe was tortured by algebra
At Archbishop Weber High School but
He never needed algebra to run the tavern.
His crank-operated adding machine lasted
Many years and did not even use electricity.

In fact—and here he imagined himself
Speaking to Alfred North Whitehead—
Joe would extend Whitehead's thinking
And require no math instruction at all
Past basic fractions and decimals.

All through the night he read, pondering,
Considering and re-considering, accepting
Many of Whitehead's ideas, questioning
Others, rejecting nothing out of hand though
Some passages caused him to stamp his foot.

Finally, as dawn broke over the university,
Joe sighed and shut the Mentor paperback.
He then noticed a name—Karen Schmolke—
Lightly inscribed by some dying ballpoint
On the front cover of *The Dialogues*.

Schmolke, Schmolke. . . Joe stroked his chin
Not an uncommon name on the Northwest Side
And here on the South Side more Schmolkes

Might be found. Should he return the book?
'Schmolke' would be in the phone directory.

But no, by God. He would keep the book.
It was a gift. It was now his prized possession.
Phrases like, 'In the nimbus of religious awe,'
Which Whitehead used so gracefully,
Made one forget he was a mathematician.

Joe's studies went on. Months passed and
He spoke to no one. He ate tuna fish.
He ordered pizza pies. Physically
He diminished. Like a breeze through the trees
His sixtieth birthday went.

Yet he felt strong and growing stronger.
The Dialogues whetted his appetite
For more Whitehead. With difficulty,
Sometimes pounding his head on the wall,
He read *Treatise on Universal Algebra*.

'*The process of forming a synthesis between*
A and B and then to consider A and B united,
As a third thing, may be symbolized as AB.'
As Joe's familiarity with Whitehead grew,
The significance of this proposition awed him.

How striking that even in the *Treatise*,
His earliest work, Whitehead referred to *AB*
As symbolic of process rather than product.
Yet the *Treatise* came thirty years before
Whitehead's greatest book, *Process and Reality*.

On and on he read. The vigor with which he
Once devoured Sidney Sheldon's *Rage of Angels*
Now energized his attack on Gottlob Frege's
Die Grundlagen der Arithmetik which he read
Using Langensheidt's German-English dictionary.

For Joe, October of 1962 was noteworthy
Not for the so-called Cuban missile crisis
But for his completion of Ernest Nagel's
Problems in the Logic of Explanation.
He found Nagel's easy style appealing.

No sooner had he finished Nagel
Than a still greater dreadnought hove
Into view. *The Structure of Scientific Revolutions*
By Thomas Samuel Kuhn made Nagel
Look like a Sunday school picnic.

One midnight—or was it noon?—night
And day were now indistinguishable—

Joe in his reading came upon a name
That, like no other, would inspire and
Instruct him for many months to come.

The name was Alonzo Church. Who was
Church? Well-known, but not well-known.
Very well-known in the world of philosophical
Mathematicians and mathematical philosophers
But unknown in most Chicago neighborhoods.

Something about Church captured Joe's fancy.
Perhaps Church's theorem on the undecidability
Of first-order logic (extending Gödel's
Incompleteness proof of 1931) engaged Joe's
Sense of himself as an intellectual outsider.

Church—like Jack Brickhouse celebrating
White Owl Wallops—was an appreciator
of Gödel, but his appreciation was such that
Church's connoisseurship and Gödel's creation
Actually fused. This was Joe's hope for himself.

He phoned for a pizza pie and took stock
Of his life. Whitehead, Nagel, Kuhn, Church—
His understanding was real even if only he
Knew it. Just like the tree falling in the forest.
Which still falls though no one hears.

His room—austere, ascetic—this was how
Wittgenstein lived. Little furniture but
The air abuzz with energy of intellect.
He would die here. He would die happy.
There was a knock on the door: the pizza.

He opened the door and it was one of those
So-called "deer in the headlights" moments,
But since that trope would not achieve
Currency for some years Joe thought of it
Differently. He thought he was fit to be tied.

Yes, he was fit to be tied. 'Schmolke?'
He inquired, diffidently. And then with
Much greater force: 'Karen Schmolke!
Delivering pizza?' He quoted Shakespeare:
'Confusion hath made his masterpiece.'

She was frightened. 'You know my name?'
Then, laughter: 'Are you psychic or what?
Here's your pie, cheese and pepperoni.
And yeah, I'm doing deliveries, man.
Life takes dough just like pizza.'

The pizza changed hands and Joe stared
Blankly at the box as Karen Schmolke stated,
'Four ninety-five plus tip. Hey, are we old friends?

Wait a minute. I know you. I gave you
A book in the Pegasus coffee house.'

'Yes, absolutely,' Joe said and quoted Buddha:
'What you have given will always be yours.'
He reached in his pocket, found a five,
Then found another five and gave her both.
'I'm so grateful to you. Please come in.'

She entered, saw his table piled high
With books and papers, his telephone
For ordering pizza, and in a corner
His mattress. 'Nice place,' she quipped,
But her sarcasm was wasted on Joe Adamczyk.

Mole-like, or like a digging aardvark
He was attacking a seemingly random
Hodgepodge of books that in his own mind
Was superbly organized, and from this
He soon retrieved Whitehead's *Dialogues*.

'Look familiar?' he said, grinning triumphantly.
Karen Schmolke nodded: 'You read it?'
The question insulted Joe: 'Of course.'
But now her attention was drawn to a paper
On the card table. 'Look! Alonzo Church!'

It was Church's June 1940 review of
Are There Extra-Syllogistic Forms of Reasoning?
By S.W. Hartman from the *Journal of Symbolic Logic*,
Joe obtained it from the John Crear Science Library
Where zeal for learning won him borrowing privileges.

'I called him Uncle Alonzo,' Karen Schmolke said.
'When Uncle Alonzo taught at the U of C,
He and my dad would sit at the kitchen table
Working on the *Entscheidungsproblem*
And I drew pictures of them with mustaches.'

'You knew Alonzo Church?' Joe urgently
Demanded—and then, as if to answer himself,
He shouted, 'You knew Alonzo Church!'
Recovering, he pointed out with reverence,
'Church was the teacher of Alan Turing.'

'Yes, he was.' said Karen Schmolke.
'He also taught Barkley Rosser and Isaac Malitz.
Dad took me to Uncle Alonzo's lectures
But at ten or eleven years old I had no interest
In the "Philosophical underpinnings of arithmetic."'

As she began a narrative of her undergraduate
Years at Oberlin College, Joe Adamczyk with an

Impatient wave, as if shooing away a horsefly,
Cut her off and with fierce interest demanded,
'What kind of lecturer was Alonzo Church?'

'Well, he had a very careful, deliberate style,'
Karen Schmolke reminisced. 'He would start
Writing on the left side of the blackboard
In a large, clear, cursive hand. . . .' She paused.
'Are you all right? Have some pizza.'

'Pizza?' said Joe distractedly, for the word
Meant nothing to him now. With the clarity
Of inner vision he saw Alonzo Church
At the blackboard, he saw Alonzo Church
Pacing around a lectern deep in thought.

And this girl Karen Schmolke! With her own
Ears she heard Alonzo Church lecture on the
Church-Turing Thesis, the Frege-Church
Ontology, the Church-Rosser theorem, and
Many similar matters. With her own ears!

For her part, Karen Schmolke just stared
In quiet puzzlement at this peculiar man
Whose name she had still not learned,
This odd duck who with his head cocked
Seemed to hear some far-off supernal music.

‘Please try some pizza,’ she offered again,
Now more insistently—for Joe’s face seemed
To be changing, his expression deepening.
What did he see? With his obvious interest
In logic, she surmised it was some esoteric proof.

But no, it was Grandma Fogarty! Oh God,
Grandma Fogarty had dropped by unexpectedly!
Joe Adamczyk felt the presence of Grandma Fogarty
And indeed he felt the presence of Grandma Fogarty
More strongly than ever in his life before!

Turning his gaze toward Karen Schmolke,
He wondered whether she might also sense
The arrival of Grandma Fogarty. Gently,
Hesitantly, he reached toward Karen Schmolke.
He caressed her cheek, then took her hand.

Wow, she thought. All men were the same.
On the other hand, never had Karen Schmolke
Felt such . . . desire? Or was it desperate need?
It was flattering, in a way. She smiled benignly.
‘It’s okay,’ she said. ‘Just don’t have a stroke.’

Her acquiescence, her mercy, these Joe chose
To see as acceptance, as heartfelt assent
When hand in hand they approached the mattress.

She wore no bra and this to Joe Adamczyk
Was a powerful expression of youth's *sans souci*.

But was there not also a *sans souci* of age?
An insouciance, a devil may care perspective,
A what the hell attitude, a damn the torpedoes
Point of view? Yes, yes, yes, goddamnit!
And Joe embraced that *carpe diem* sensibility!

He gamahuched Karen Schmolke with startling
Enthusiasm. Cunt, slut and similar words
Eddied and swirled in his brain. Yet a *logos*,
A *telos*, was also disclosing itself, cleverly
Interweaving his fucking with philosophy.

Through this most intimate touching
Of a woman who had seen Alonzo Church,
Joe felt himself connected not just to Church
But through Church to the realm of pure forms
Described by Pythagoras, Plato, and others.

Thought and feeling, cunt and consequentialism,
Mingled until an aphorism of Whitehead's emerged:
'There are no whole truths. All truths are half-truths,'
The great man explained. That is: truth is never final,
Truth is ever on the way, always halfway there.

Like Achilles' fabled pursuit of the tortoise
Truth is a reality but a reality of process.
Truly Joe had been a bartender. Just as truly
He was one no longer. Who could aver that he
Would not one day be President of Mexico?

Rising to his knees, he poised his swollen member
To enter Karen Schmolke. She arched her back
And her breasts like spring lambs leaped to meet him
Until for at least a moment his ratiocinations quieted
And twice she nutted to one nut of Joe Adamczyk's.

I hope you have enjoyed this story of a man who
Late in life undertook what Alfred North Whitehead
Called *Adventures of Ideas* and then, to his surprise,
Reignited his sexuality, which he called Grandma Fogarty.
And Eve Grabuskawa? Her story will be told, but not today.

2013

Afterword

As a freshman at Columbia, intoxicated by poetry, I joined the *Columbia Review*, headquarters for a clever and heady bunch of literati who had studied with Kenneth Koch and were big converts to the New York School of poetry before anyone else had heard of it. Outsiders said the magazine was run as a "clique," which is probably true but may also account for its particular excellence. Among the *Review* contributors in the 1960s were Ron Padgett, Philip Lopate, David Shapiro, and Paul Auster among others who have achieved renown.

Of the staff members on the magazine when I joined up, Mitch Sisskind was the one whose judgment everyone respected the most. He had tremendous talent, and at meetings, whether formal or impromptu, you could count on his candor and on his ability to see the humor in things.

I valued every minute with Mitch, who was three years my senior and seemed infinitely wiser to the ways of the world. On the night when the police forcibly evicted the student protestors who had seized Avery Hall and four other campus buildings in April 1968, he and I supped on sandwiches at the West End Bar before taking our places among those who were willing to interpose our bodies between the cops and the militants inside. It was a tense moment. Kenneth Koch stood in the faculty cordon right in front of us. Mitch recited the 23rd Psalm and Thomas Wyatt's "They Flee from Me" as we waited for officers of the TPF—the Tactical Patrol Force—to rush at us swinging their sticks.

The Columbia "Poem Team" was Mitch's idea. A bunch of us drove to Sarah Lawrence, Vassar, and Mount Holyoke—to women's colleges exclusively, Columbia at the time being all male—and read our stories or poems. The Columbia administration supported the effort with funds to cover gas and tolls. (Because I was the most conventional looking of the group and made dean's list, I was drafted to pitch the idea to associate dean Erwin Glikes, who approved.) Mitch even wrote a curious manifesto, which began with the proclamation that "a poem is not as valuable as a sheep."

One time Mitch and another fellow were sitting on the ledge facing Ferris Booth Hall, which was then the student activities center with an auditorium, a bowling alley, ping-pong tables, and the Lion's Den, a café where you could eat hamburgers, drink coffee, and listen to the Supremes sing "You Keep Me Hanging On." The fellow took a poem out of his pocket and showed it to Mitch, who read it, handed it back, and said, "Not one of your major works." That line was used pretty regularly after that.

Mitch wrote a wonderful series of one-line poems that started with one entitled "I am the Toilet." The line: "Dance on, you pigs. I will never get used to it."

In Spring '68 the guys at the *Review* published a mimeographed daily that bore some sort of relation to the campus-wide protests over the war in Vietnam and the building of a local gymnasium—but *Janet Benderman*, as it was called, was more frankly a blasphemously comic ode to the gods of chance than a political statement in any ordinary sense. The editors wanted to run one of Mitch's one-liners each day. But his typed copy—this was before Xerox machines were routine—was lost. All that was left was the memory of a second title: "Cardinal Spellman's Big Day." So the editors dutifully published this title with the same line as before: "Dance on, you pigs. I will never get used to it." I think Mitch got the line from Kafka.

Mitch had a poem called "More and More Lady Bird," and all these years later I still get a kick out of "Ah really like you as a person, Premier Ngox," which makes fun of LBJ not only in the mangling of the Vietnamese name but in the phrase "as a person." It was an idiotic phrase you would never use after reading this poem.

Of the poems Mitch published in *Columbia Review* back then, my favorite is "I Worked for the Old Central Electric Company," a takeoff on the kind of speech made when a long-time employee steps down. The poem manages to lampoon nostalgia and achieve it simultaneously thanks to the writer's ironic restraint, the deadpan tone that extends even to the exclamation point following the comparison of a hole-in-one in golf to a triple play in baseball. (I am quite proudly going on memory.) At Columbia, Mitch played lightweight football and produced a radio program about the "Monsters of the Midway," the fabled Chicago Bears' teams that were quarterbacked by Sid Luckman, a Columbia alum, and he always wrote about professional sports with precision, as in his poem consisting entirely of wrestling holds, "A Wrist Lock."

Mitch's imagination is anarchic, perhaps prophetic and, in at least one instance, biblical. I am not certain when it occurred to Mitch that the Columbia campus might be just the right place for a reprise of the ten plagues God visited upon the stiff-necked Egyptians in Exodus. The first plague, blood, presented difficulties, but Mitch managed to order a shipment of frogs (the second plague), which he planned to unleash. Did he? My memory fails me here.

Of the early stories, I have an enduring fondness for "A Mean Teacher" and its gorgeous ending, as beautiful as it is funny. I was there when Mitch first read the story aloud. And I remember other readings, some more recent, and would wager that there are more brilliant works lurking out there than this canny writer is letting on.

A born storyteller, alert to the comic possibilities of a situation, Mitch is a master of dialects and of speech patterns, like the drill instructor in an early story who can "guran-fucken-tee you" an unpleasant outcome. He has a special feeling for the cities of Chicago, where he grew up; New York, where he spent time in college and after; and Los Angeles, where he resides and drives. Several of his poems have appeared in *The Best American Poetry*. "Like a Monkey" was a highlight of the 2009 edition.

Mitch circulates poems and stories among friends but has done little to advance his literary reputation or pursue publication. Thus his writing is something of a secret and has all the virtues that this implies: Mitch Sisskind writes to honor no one's muse but his own, and as a result his work stands out in any crowd for its originality and authenticity. There is deep feeling and a moral instinct here, however much the sentiment may conceal itself in irony—and sadness may take the disguise of laughter. Though you can never count on history to make the right judgments, I can't help feeling that the rest of the world will catch up and recognize the genius of this extraordinary writer.

DAVID LEHMAN

OTHER TITLES FROM THE SONG CAVE

1. *A Dark Dreambox of Another Kind* by **Alfred Starr Hamilton**
2. *My Enemies* by **Jane Gregory**
3. *Rude Woods* by **Nate Klug**
4. *Georges Braque and Others* by **Trevor Winkfield**
5. *The Living Method* by **Sara Nicholson**
6. *Splash State* by **Todd Colby**
7. *Essay Stanzas* by **Thomas Meyer**
8. *Illustrated Games of Patience* by **Ben Estes**
9. *Dark Green* by **Emily Hunt**
10. *Honest James* by **Christian Schlegel**
11. *M* by **Hannah Brooks-Motl**
12. *What the Lyric Is* by **Sara Nicholson**
13. *The Hermit* by **Lucy Ives**
14. *The Orchid Stories* by **Kenward Elmslie**